COUNT COLLIN VAN REENAN

# THE SPACES IN BETWEEN

Published by RedDoor
www.reddoorpublishing.com

ISBN 978-1-910453-48-3

Cover design: Patrick Knowles
www.patrickknowlesdesign.com

Illustrations on pages xvi and xvii drawn
by Graham Larwood
Plans on page 12 provided by Danny Hope of Hope
Design Studio Ltd

Typesetting: Tutis Innovative E-Solutions Pte. Ltd

Print managed by Jellyfish Solutions Ltd

*To Sue, without whom nothing would be possible*

'Every man has reminiscences which he would not tell to everyone, but only to his friends.

'He has other matters in his mind which he would not reveal even to his friends, but only to himself, and that in secret.

'But there are other things that a man is afraid to tell, even to himself, and every decent man has a number of such things stored away in his mind.'

Dostoevsky, *Notes from the Underground*

*Some people may consider this is a ghost story; others, like my father, a crime. Some would say that it describes the relentless descent into neurosis; others that it is the greatest love story they know.*

Marie-Claire Gröller, Paris, 1970

# Preface

*'This is one of those cases in which the imagination is baffled
by the facts.'*

Winston Churchill

My name is Marie-Claire Gröller, Doctor of Psychiatry.
I deal with the neurotic, the psychotic and even the
psychopathic, and I have many strange tales to tell; but none
so utterly mysterious as the facts related in the following pages.

Normally (not a word that figures often in my profession),
the rules of patient confidentiality would prevent such a story
from ever leaving my files. There are, however, exceptions. In
the case of dire need of the patient and with his full consent, it
may be permitted to publish such details in the desperate hope
that it may bring relief and closure for him.

In this case the patient is, moreover, also my friend.

His steadily deteriorating condition has forced me to
take these unusual steps. Someone, somewhere, knows what
happened, and could, if he or she had the courage to come
forward, bring some sort of respite to a man who has suffered a
great wrong and who is slowly sinking under the despair of not
knowing why.

I first met the man (whom I shall call Nicholas) in late October 1968. After I qualified from the Sorbonne in Paris and spent two years at the Pitié-Salpêtrière Hospital, in 1968 my parents helped me to open my own practice in a small town called Rueil-Malmaison, about fifteen minutes by car from the centre of Paris to the north-west, across the Seine and behind the beautiful Bois de Boulogne Park. The town was already well served by consultants in all aspects of medicine, and at first I struggled to find work. Patients are most often referred to psychiatrists by general practitioners, and they preferred established and experienced colleagues. There was also, at that time, a certain amount of prejudice against women in the medical profession.

Fortunately, a young doctor close to my own practice was very helpful to me (we later married) and sent me my first patient.

My father was a *commissaire de police*, a high rank in the *police judiciaire*, and used part of his retirement pension to set me up in practice. My *cabinet* or practice was rather humble, consisting simply of two rooms above a lingerie boutique on the Rue Paul Vaillant-Couturier, a few yards from the church where the Empress Joséphine is entombed. The first room, furnished only with a desk and filing cabinet, served as the reception, and the second, with just two armchairs and a small table, as my practice room. I had to act as my own receptionist and answer the telephone to make appointments.

It was nearly a week before I received my first call. Dr David wished to refer a young man. The patient claimed he was suffering from insomnia, but the doctor suspected he was in fact clinically depressed. This young man, who lived nearby, was not registered locally with any doctor and had asked Dr David merely for a prescription for sleeping tablets. However, his appearance, lack of appetite and general state of health suggested to the good doctor that the problem was in the mind rather than the body. Dr David warned me that, although his new patient had reluctantly agreed to see me, he was very reticent and wary when asked about his background.

Trying not to sound too eager, I arranged an appointment, and 10 a.m. the next day found me peeping surreptitiously through the blinds on the street side of my rooms. When the bell sounded, I felt a childlike and inappropriate excitement, and wondered if perhaps I should be consulting someone myself!

Heart racing, I admitted my first private patient and led the way upstairs.

It was only when we found ourselves next to my two armchairs that I really had a chance to look at my client. He waited politely for me to sit, and that gave me a chance to observe him. My first impressions were of a man about twenty-three or twenty-four years of age, of medium height and build. I also noted that he was wearing an expensive, elegant if rather shabby dark grey suit, beautifully cut but in a rather old-fashioned double-breasted style, which seemed to hang on him as though he had lost some weight since it was made. Unusually for the times, his hair was short – brown, wavy, but with some premature greying at the sides. The shape of his face, together with his fair complexion, suggested that he was a northern European. His deep-set grey eyes were ringed with dark shadows that suggested lack of sleep.

Uneasy at my perhaps too obvious scrutiny, he fidgeted, eyes on the floor; but then he looked up suddenly with a shy smile and I glimpsed – again unusually for those heavy-smoking, coffee-drinking times – perfect white teeth.

Introducing myself and explaining Dr David's concern, I asked him outright if anything was troubling him. He fidgeted uneasily again and refused to meet my eyes. Finally, he said that he was unable to sleep well, following an 'unsettling experience' a few months previously. His appetite also seemed to have deserted him and he felt unable to relax. He lived alone and was currently unemployed, living on an allowance sent to him by his parents.

As I listened to his soft voice, I noted that his French was clear and his pronunciation precise – an educated French that was, I thought, very good. In fact too good; I was listening to someone who was not speaking his mother tongue. I looked again at the name on the file I had just created – 'Nicholas Van R.' – and assumed that I was dealing with a Belgian, from Flanders. When I enquired, however, he told me that he was in fact English, though his mother was Irish and his father's family had connections in South Africa.

I continued to probe and learned that he had come to Paris aged thirteen because his mother wanted him to be educated in France. At first he had boarded at the Lycée Henri-IV, afterwards spending a couple of years at the University of Liège, Belgium, where he had relatives, and then about two years ago had started a humanities course at the Sorbonne, with the intention of becoming a journalist. The first year, he had studied existentialism under Professor Paul Genestier, whom he greatly admired, but in his second year his tuition was taken over by Professor Robert S.– H.–, who, although he treated him well, was not someone Nicholas had been able to warm to.

He stopped suddenly and looked up at me; again that shy smile.

'You were going to tell me about your "unsettling experience"…' I prompted.

'Well…' He hesitated. 'I'm not actually sure it's relevant…'

'Please go on.' I smiled back. I could see we were getting closer to the problem and I needed to keep the momentum going.

He was uncomfortable now and again refused to look at me. When he was not smiling, his face appeared gaunt, and the dark shadows around his eyes made him look older than his years.

'Please… Nicholas, if I may call you that… I can't help you if you don't explain…'

Slowly, he began to resume his story.

'Well, it all started to go wrong – for me, that is – just at the start of January of this year. My parents retired to South Africa, but for some complicated reason their bank accounts were frozen…some business court case, I was told. Suddenly, my allowance stopped. I didn't have much in the way of savings but I found some evening work as a *plongeur* in various restaurants and was just about managing…by making all sorts of economies. But…'

He looked up at me.

'But I didn't have a work permit and, when my student visa expired in March, I didn't have the funds to show to get it renewed. I was unhappy with my classes…I hadn't taken to Professor S.– H.–, as I said, and I had problems meeting my rent. The final straw was the outbreak of the student riots in May. There was a lot of damage…the restaurants closed and I could no longer earn money. I lost my rooms and had to doss down with friends…I even stayed with the Professor, just for a few days, that's how desperate I was. I think I lived on *cafés au lait* for a couple of weeks. Then –'

He stopped abruptly, and it was obvious that he was approaching something that made him uncomfortable.

'Please go on, Nicholas. I'm here to listen.'

He looked hard at me, as if trying to decide whether he could trust me, looked down at the floor and then, very slowly, raised his eyes to mine, made his decision and began, haltingly, 'Then Bruno…a friend…found an ad in *Le Figaro*…for an

English tutor…to live in. It seemed the only answer…the police were after me for overstaying my visa – you know, they threw all the foreign students out after the riots. Well, anyway, I took the job…in this really strange house…with an even weirder family.'

He stopped again and I was shocked to see tears running down his face.

'And then – then that's when it started.'

He stopped, unable to speak, and to hide his embarrassment stared rigidly at the floor. It was obvious to me that if I pressed him further it would only be detrimental to his confidence.

After a while, I said gently, 'Look, Nicholas, I hope to be able to help you but I need to know the full details. I can't promise you a "quick fix" but we have plenty of time. I'd like you to make another appointment to continue our chat –'

'I don't think I can talk about it, doctor…' he broke in, agitated. 'It's too long and complicated and you won't believe me anyway – no one does.'

I could see there was no point in continuing right now, so I suggested a tried and tested, if unimaginative, approach.

'Well, Nicholas, we will meet again next week, and in the meantime I would like you to write down all the details. Write it *all* down. It's important that you don't leave anything out. Do you understand?'

He nodded without looking up.

'Now, has Dr David given you any medication?'

He shook his head.

'OK. I'm going to prescribe something for you, just a mild sedative, but you must try to eat regularly and get plenty of exercise and fresh air. Do we have a deal?'

He smiled a little sadly and stood up, thanking me.

From the window, I watched him leave the building and wander down the street in the direction of the church.

My first patient. I knew it was going to be quite a challenge, but nothing could have prepared me for what eventually followed.

Suddenly, my practice took off. In the week following that first session with Nicholas, I had a consultation practically every day, and I confess that I gave little thought to his case. So when he turned up the following Friday I had to consult my notes hurriedly before I called him through.

He looked tired and drawn, and once again ill at ease. It occurred to me that there must be a woman involved in this, perhaps unrequited love; but, whatever it was, I suspected that having a woman as his psychiatrist might be something he was finding difficult.

The battered folder he put down in front of me looked suspiciously thin for a summary of his 'unsettling experiences' over a period of almost six weeks, and I began to doubt the wisdom of asking him to write them down. Perhaps a series of interview sessions would have induced him eventually to be more forthcoming.

I made no comment, though, and took the folder with good grace. As I looked up suddenly, I caught him looking at me, studying me, as it were, as though trying to make up his mind to trust me. It convinced me even more that there was a woman at the bottom of all this – '*cherchez la femme*', as we say. He smiled to hide his embarrassment at being caught out, and I felt instinctively that I had passed some sort of a test for him, perhaps by not commenting on the brevity of the folder, and that he accepted me. It was a turning point in our relationship and I hoped his newfound trust would help him open up to me.

The manuscript was a huge disappointment. Even a cursory glance proved that. A series of dates and a short recounting of 'facts'; it was just like a police witness statement – a report of an incident, ten pages of facts with no feeling, no personal observation, nothing at all to help me.

Deciding to test his confidence in our relationship, I pointedly closed the file, looked up at him and held his eyes, forcing him to look at me.

'I'm sorry, Nicholas; this is not at all what I had in mind. It's a legal dossier – a list of events; I want to know how you *felt*, what you thought, how you reacted. I want a blow-by-blow account of your emotions, your intimate perception of these events…'

He looked shocked that I should suggest such a thing.

'Nicholas, I need to see inside your head. I'm a mind doctor, not a mind-reader: I can't guess how you felt then, or feel now. You have to *tell* me. You said you wanted to be a writer, so use your talent, Nicholas, and don't come back till you've written it all down for me.'

I knew it was a calculated risk; he might not come back at all. But I had to take a chance on that, or I could not help him.

I did not see Nicholas for several weeks. Nobody did. He locked himself away in his tiny flat in Rueil-Malmaison and – he told me later – just wrote and wrote until he had it all down on paper.

When he delivered it, his physical appearance so shocked me that I sent him back to Dr David for an urgent check-up; I thought he might be suffering from exhaustion. He was eventually persuaded to join some friends on a short trip to Italy.

It took me several hours to read Nicholas's account, and it had a profound effect on me. At first, I thought it a romance, and then perhaps a crime thriller and, finally, a ghost story.

It follows here, in its entirety, with no changes except the correction of a few archaic grammatical expressions and slightly old-fashioned idioms. His French also contains one or two student slang expressions which I have changed to avoid confusion. Throughout his account, Nicholas has varied people's first names, sometimes using the French form, i.e. Natalie, and sometimes the Russian, Natalya; likewise Serge and Sergei. I have seen no point in standardising these, as the sense is always evident. When unusual Russian words have been used, an explanation is given.

It is a strange and harrowing story.

Madame Lili

Her Imperial Highness, Princess Natalya

# Nicholas's Story

# CHAPTER 1

# Unrest

*'Ce n'est pas une révolution, Sire, c'est une mutation.'*

SLOGAN, MAY 1968

The few francs that I had were long since spent and a Métro ticket was out of the question; so when the tube stopped at Place St-Michel I dodged the automatic barrier by going through behind another student, glued to his back and barging him forward so as not to get caught in the closing door. He knew but he didn't even turn round; I mean, we all did it in those days.

My mind was buzzing as we trooped up the steps of the exit. What would it be like, the Boulevard St-Michel, after nearly two weeks of student riots? Would the trees still be standing? Would the fountain be running? Would all the shop windows be smashed?

I was so lost in thought that I didn't see him until it was too late and he'd seen me first. To go back down would have been too obvious, so I kept on up the steps and tried to look casual.

He was a few years older than I; twenty-six or twenty-eight perhaps, short hair, clean-shaven and wearing a very smart dark suit. It was a fine spring day in mid-May and the sun shone on the last few steps. But I felt a sudden chill.

I tried not to make eye contact but I could feel him looking at me, and when I came level with him on the top step he pushed his police ID right into my face. '*Police nationale, monsieur. Sûreté. Renseignments Généraux!*' He paused for effect and then spat out the words, '*Pièces d'identité. PAPIERS!*'

Police checks were nothing new to me; unused to such things at home in England, I had at first found them daunting, but as a student in Paris I had soon become inured to the process. But today I was afraid. Afraid because my visa had expired, afraid because I had no money, and afraid because the police were far from happy with students.

'*Bonjour, Monsieur l'Inspecteur,*' I stammered, and made a gesture as if to search my pockets for the sacred 'papers'. I needed to explain my situation as quickly as possible. '*Vous voyez, monsieur, le problème, c'est que –*'

I didn't get a chance to finish. The back of his hand hit me smack on the left cheek and I staggered back, blinking, nearly falling back down the steps to the Métro.

'*Papiers, et que ça saute!*' He hissed. Papers, and jump to it!

I thought of hanging a right hook on his chin and dismissed the idea instantly; even if I survived the subsequent beating, French prisons are hell. So I said nothing and did not resist as he dragged me across the pavement to the '*panier à salade*' parked in the nearby Rue de la Huchette. The van was already half full; a few *clochards* (tramps) and the rest students like me. Some bore the marks of earlier encounters, and I thought myself lucky to get off with just a hard slap – so far at least. Conversation was forbidden and shortly after, we were driven to the *commissariat* of the IVème *arrondissement*, across the river on the right bank, and 'interviewed' there.

I got lucky: my interviewer was an old inspector who I guessed was already retired and had been brought back to help out during this time of unrest. He had nothing to prove and had long since had his fill of violence; more to the point, he had spent some time in London and was something of an Anglophile, so I told him everything – the truth. It wasn't complicated: how I came to be there, where I was studying, what I was studying. Then I explained that my funds had been held up and that I couldn't find work because of the student riots. I assured him that it was only temporary and that I would soon receive some money and renew my student visa…basically, anything I thought might help my case.

I thought he seemed sympathetic, but my hopes came crashing down when he said they were taking me to the Gare du Nord and would put me on a train back to Calais and then England. But, when I got into the car, he sort of winked at me. At the station, he took me to the platform and on to the Calais train and then turned, looked hard at me, and walked away.

It took several seconds for it to dawn on me, and then I wasted no time in getting off the train and walking back into the station to lose myself in the crowds. This time I walked to St-Michel and, after checking that the police control was no longer in place, cut off down the side streets to the little café we all frequented.

The walk was depressing: beautiful trees had been felled across the Boul'Mich and dozens of street-sweepers were out clearing the broken glass from the shop windows. Some of the barricades had not yet been dismantled, and here and there small groups of helmeted CRS in their long black rubber coats stood chatting and smoking. In one or two places I caught a whiff of tear gas, and there were blood spatters on the pavements.

The café appeared to be closed. There were no lights on and the windows were completely obscured by condensation. The door opened, though, and I saw Max and Aurélie sitting in the corner. Apart from them, the place was empty, the chairs piled upon the tables, the floor unswept and littered with dog-ends.

Behind the counter, Jean-Marie nodded a greeting and a flick of his eyebrows asked the question.

'I've no money, Jean-Marie,' I said. '*Que dalle!*' Broke.

He shrugged and set the coffee machine in motion.

Max kept his eyes closed as I sat down. Aurélie looked up briefly and then went back to rolling a cigarette, one of the thin, dark tobacco ones wrapped in liquorice paper that she smoked endlessly. We had had a bit of a 'thing' going once, for a short time, a while before. She was quite attractive in a bohemian way, slim, with elfin features and short blonde hair.

But Aurélie wasn't interested in how she looked. She didn't need to attract a man – she was married to the Revolution – a sort of sixties version of the women who knitted while the heads from the guillotine rolled into the basket. She mumbled endlessly about student power, people power, the Left, Jacques Sauvageot, Alain Geismar, Daniel (Dany le Rouge) Cohn-Bendit; she knew them all, or so she said. She was really a doctor's daughter from St-Germain-en-Laye and was in revolt about that, along with everything else. This morning she looked terrible: great dark lines under her eyes, her hair matted and uncombed and her pretty, even teeth stained by nicotine and black coffee. She was wearing a shapeless pink woollen dress pulled in by a wide belt and with a huge, baggy rolled collar.

I leaned across the table and kissed her on each cheek but she didn't look up, and I noticed that she had been neglecting her personal hygiene as much as her appearance. Still, she droned on about the Revolution, the CRS, Fouchet and the Gaullists – a never-ending monologue that did not require any input from me, or anyone else for that matter. Just as well, because French politics left me cold. I just couldn't get excited about it all; these people were obsessed with revolutions and they kept restoring the 'Old Order' so they could have another revolution to replace it. I mean, five republics should be enough for anyone! It was a national pastime that I just could not get enthusiastic about.

Jean-Marie came over to our table carrying a huge bowl of milky coffee and a croissant to break into it. I'd been living on this stuff for nearly a week.

'I've no money,' I said again, but he just shrugged and slammed it down in front of me. That was the ambivalence of the Parisians – mean to the last centime of a bill, generous to a fault the next moment.

Max opened his eyes and looked up at me, at the coffee, at Aurélie, and then closed his eyes again and shrank lower into the duffel-coat arrangement that he lived in. His life veered from intense, almost frenetic energy to total lethargy. He could sleep almost anywhere and made a most unlikely *carabin*, or medical student. He had an astute brain, though, and could often beat me in a discussion. He was usually in funds, but he didn't offer it around.

So there we sat. No other customers. It was so quiet. The felled trees kept the Boul'Mich and the Boulevard St-Germain barred to traffic, and few people ventured out through the debris of the previous night's riots.

I closed my eyes and drifted off for a few seconds, to the accompaniment of Aurélie's monologue and the slight wheezing noise coming from Max's open mouth.

The slamming of the door and a gust of fresh air woke me in time to see Bruno's huge frame ambling towards us, lugging a battered suitcase that I realised, with foreboding, was mine. He greeted Aurélie with a kiss, took a look at the still-sleeping Max and, sitting down, stored the suitcase under the table and shook hands with Jean-Marie and myself, all in a series of high speed manoeuvres. Then he grinned at me.

I liked Bruno the best of all my student friends, a huge, bluff, easygoing lad 'of peasant stock' as they say. But what he may have lacked in sophistication he made up for with his frank and open disposition. Engineering was his passion, but for some reason he preferred the company of humanities students and had attached himself to us within days of arriving in Paris from his home village near Metz. Bruno was a thoroughly decent guy and had allowed me to sleep on the couch in his room for the last week or so. So why the suitcase?

'Want the good news or the bad news?' He continued to grin.

'It's *all* bad, isn't it?

'Not at all, Nico, old son. The bad bit is that you've got to vacate my room. The landlord's found out about it and he's threatening to chuck me out.'

I stared at him as my sluggish brain took in this latest disaster. Finally, I asked, 'So what's the good news?'

'I've found you a job, or sort of…'

Max opened his eyes and asked, 'A job? What, Nico?'

Bruno nodded, pleased with the reaction he was getting. From deep inside his coat, he extracted a crumpled scrap of paper and slapped it down on the table, where it proceeded to soak up the slops of Aurélie's spilled coffee. Snatching it up again, Bruno smoothed it carefully on a dry corner of the table and then pushed it over to me.

It appeared to be a blurry photocopy of the employment page of *Le Figaro*. Halfway down one column, an inch of print had been circled with a red pen. Bruno jabbed a thick finger at it excitedly. 'There, it's you to a T, Nico! Could solve all your problems, *mon pote.*'

Aurélie snatched it up and read it out loud. '*Native English-speaker wanted to tutor 17-year-old at home three days per week. Must speak French. Knowledge of Russian useful. Three months' renewable contract, board and lodging, generous salary.*'

I stared at Bruno. 'What on earth…?'

'No, listen, Nico. Think about it for a moment. Board and lodging, right? Generous salary, right? Native English-speaker, must speak French, right?'

'And Russian, Bruno, what about that?'

'You speak Russian, Nico. I heard you with that bloke who lives next to me…'

'That's Polish, and anyway, it's only a few phrases I picked up…'

'Nah, Nico, you speak *all* the languages – that's what you do, isn't it? Listen, it's only for three months. Somewhere to sleep, something to eat, better pay than washing-up, loads of spare time to study. And, you won't miss much at the Sorbonne: it's all closed up now and it will be at least a couple of months before things get back to normal. Plus the fact that you'll be out of the way of the police checks, and then you can use your saved earnings when you apply for a new student visa.'

I opened my mouth to object, but then closed it again. What Bruno was saying actually made good sense and I didn't know why I was so reluctant to admit it.

Bruno's enthusiasm seemed suddenly to desert him and I felt that my ingratitude had hurt him. I couldn't even offer him a cup of coffee.

Aurélie, rolling yet another cigarette, looked up at me, questions written all over her face. Max, eyes still closed, said, 'Bruno's got a point. Sounds ideal to me.'

All of them were right. I realised that. They weren't just winding me up. It did make sense. I was just reluctant to admit it. I looked at the ad again. A seventeen-year-old; that might not be so bad – I mean, it wasn't as though it was a naughty young kid. Three months wasn't so long either, and it would be nice to have somewhere to sleep properly. The food would probably be what the family ate themselves, and few Parisians ate badly. Maybe I could bullshit the Russian language bit.

'OK, I'll give it a go. Where is it?' I said, more out of bravado than confidence. 'Neuilly! Christ! That's a good Métro ride away and, anyway, I haven't got any money.'

Bruno grinned again.

'Thought of that,' he said, holding up a 'Pasteur' – a five-franc note.

I took the note, and promised to pay him back. I had to; I couldn't get out of it now. It was touching really; Bruno was the least able to give me money.

The trip up to Neuilly cost me three francs and I spent another one franc thirty on more coffee when I got to the stop. I gave no thought to how I would get back if I didn't get the job, but I did think it would seem odd to turn up carrying a suitcase, as if I was certain I would be taken on. So I left the case with the café barman and, following his directions, eventually found the address.

# Ground Floor Plans of the House

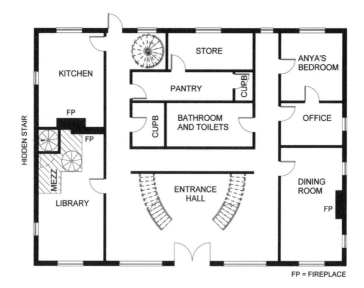

# First Floor Plans of the House

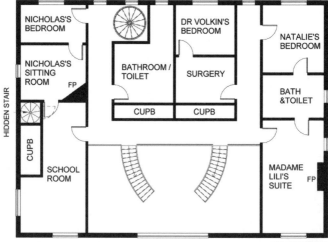

# CHAPTER 2

# The House

*'Surely such are the dwellings of the wicked, and this is the place of him that knoweth not God.'*

JOB 18:21

Although the address was correct, I had some difficulty in finding the House. Off the main boulevard, a narrow dog's-leg led between tall hedges, hiding tall, angular chalets that the French call *pavillons*, and the further I followed the *allée* the narrower it became, until it was only just wide enough to take a motor vehicle. In fact the road here was not tarmac, and tufts of grass grew up through the sandy gravel, suggesting that no car had passed this way for a very long time.

The *allée* swung left and then sharp right, and stopped again at a set of tall portal gates that had once been magnificent, no doubt, but now showed long neglect. The dark green paint was cracked and flaking, revealing mottled orange rust underneath. On a red brick pillar hung a sign, with a white *No. 4* on a chipped blue enamel background. The gates were chained together and padlocked, and I searched in vain for a way in which I could request entry. To one side, the gate had a smaller gate within it, just wide enough to admit a person on foot. It was bolted but, to my relief, not locked, and it creaked loudly as I pushed it open. A driveway, overgrown until it was little more than a wide track, lay in front of me, flanked by huge rhododendron bushes, the buds just turning pink, and I had to continue for several yards in the bright spring sunshine before rounding a bend and seeing the House for the first time.

Initially, I was disappointed. The gates, the shrub-lined drive…I suppose I was expecting to see a small but impressive *château* set in an extensive park; silly really, because this was still deep in the suburbs of Paris. Instead, I saw a three-storey stone house with steeply pitched, almost Gothic roofs, hidden by the hedges of neighbouring gardens. Close up, I could see that the building was bigger than it first appeared, being as deep as it was wide. Its most impressive features were the huge stained glass windows that reached up two floors either side of the arched double entry doors. The sun, now high in the sky, bathed the whole façade in sparkling light, and, though there was little warmth in it, seemed to give the whole house a bright and welcoming look. Had it been otherwise, I think I would have turned and walked away, since I was still far from sure that I was doing the right thing and feeling suddenly uneasy about the whole idea.

Would to God I had followed that intuition.

And so I stepped up to the old oak doors and pulled down hard on the metal handle that ran in brackets up the stone wall to the right. If a bell rang, I certainly didn't hear it, buried as it must have been in the depths of the House.

Above the door was a bronze plate with an inscription in Latin: *Taceant colloquia. Effugiat risus. Hic locus est ubi Mors gaudet succurrere Vitae.* I struggled with it and then gave up. What sort of a 'tutor' couldn't even read the sign above his pupil's house?

Later, when I did get around to translating it – *Let idle talk be silenced. Let laughter be banished. Here is the place where Death delights to succour Life* – I felt I'd missed another warning sign.

I could not be sure if anyone knew I was there, and again that uneasy feeling swept over me. I forced myself to wait long seconds but heard no movement within. With something approaching relief, I stepped down from the door and began to retrace my steps towards the gate. When I think now how close I came to getting away… I should have followed my instinct even though there was no logic in it.

'*Vous désirez, monsieur?*'

A male voice, hoarse and rough, sounded behind me and, turning, I came face to face with the strangest man. Standing in the open door was an old guy somewhere in his fifties, very tall and slim, in a rangy sort of way, his skin deeply lined, with iron-grey crew-cut hair against a brownish, weatherbeaten face. A huge white nicotine-stained moustache hung beneath a hawkish nose, high cheekbones and deep-set, half-closed eyes.

He was dressed in what appeared to be riding breeches over tall, brown riding boots, with a white long-sleeved shirt buttoned down one side. A Cossack! My mind flicked back to the mention of Russian in the job advertisement.

With some reluctance, I turned and walked back towards him.

'*Vous désirez?*' he asked again, and I caught a whiff of tobacco and saddle soap.

'*La situation, monsieur…l'emploi…dans le journal…*'

He looked at me narrowly, his deep-set eyes squinting into the sunlight. After what seemed an age, he receded into the House with an abrupt, '*Entrez! Attendez ici.*' Then, almost as an afterthought, he added, '*S'il vous plaît, monsieur.*'

He disappeared, leaving me to gaze in wonderment at the scene. In front of me was a great hall with a double staircase forming a neat horseshoe up to the landing of the next floor. The sunshine streamed through the huge stained glass windows behind me, throwing a kaleidoscope of multicoloured light upon the black and white tessellated floor. To the left and right front, wide red-carpeted steps curved upwards, and either side of them were dark passages leading deep inside the House.

The sight took my breath away and, at the same time, made my uneasiness recede. The colours, the glowing warmth of the carpets, offset the cold austerity of the black and white marble floor and the heavy dark oak of the stair rails and wall panelling. A feeling of great relief came over me; a feeling of calmness and security quite unlike the taut nervousness with which I had been living for the past few weeks.

I stood rooted to the spot, trying to take it all in and get a grip on my emotions, so preoccupied that I failed to notice the return of my host. His sudden voice startled me.

'*Veuillez me suivre, monsieur. Par ici…*'

He led me to the left, through tall oak double doors and into a high book-lined room; he pointed at a leather sofa behind a low table, turned abruptly, and was gone. I approached the seat but did not sit down and just gazed around me at the hundreds of leather-bound books that reached up to a mezzanine floor, halfway up the double-storeyed room. On the low table stood a strange silver vase-like object which I eventually decided was a samovar, since around it hung small, thick drinking glasses. In spite of the spring weather, a coal fire burned in the grate of the marble fireplace and gave the room a cosier feel. I tried to read some of the titles on the book spines but most of them were in Russian script.

Turning back to face the door, I saw that a short, slim girl had entered the room and had been waiting patiently behind me. She held out her hand for me to shake.

'I'm Anya,' she said, with a broad and attractive smile. Her small, rather elfin face was framed by dark hair swept up on to the top of her head in a sort of loose bun, and I glimpsed something strange and indefinable about her eyes.

'I'm the Grand Duchess's secretary,' she continued, 'and I'm to interview those people who reply to our advertisement.'

I continued to look at this 'Anya' and suddenly understood what it was that was unusual about her eyes: her irises were different colours – one brown, one green.

Caught out staring, I offered lamely, 'Er, yes, it's about the job…er, post…'

She sat down, and motioned for me to do the same. There followed a long conversation about me, my qualifications, my background, education, etc. It seemed quite thorough, but I had the strangest feeling that she was just going through the motions. It made it easier for me to hedge about certain aspects of my CV and particularly about my immigration status. To my great relief, she didn't ask to see my passport or enquire whether I had any written references. She was very relaxed and easy to talk to and, in spite of her Slavic-sounding name, spoke excellent French, with perhaps a hint of a Belgian accent; maybe she was from the north.

Presently, Anya served me my first taste of Russian tea from the samovar that I had earlier admired, and must have picked up on my reaction to it, because she laughed and said, 'Yes, it's something of an acquired taste! Like our cigarettes.'

She left me to persevere with the tea while she made her report to the Grand Duchess, who it seemed lived upstairs and, being very old, seldom left her suite. It didn't seem very long before she returned, smiling, and told me that the post was mine. Naturally, I was a little surprised, and it crossed my mind that there might not have been that many candidates.

I looked at Anya and decided that she was really quite attractive, even with her old-style bun, lack of make-up and rather frumpish long dress. Suddenly, she smiled broadly and gave a sort of throaty laugh that somehow belied the serious rôle she had earlier assumed.

'But...' She paused; then, smiling again, 'But you should listen carefully to what I am about to say before you accept.'

The smile vanished and was replaced by a frown and a very direct look.

'There are several factors that you should consider carefully.'

She paused again, apparently for effect.

'The first concerns your pupil. Her Imperial Highness Natalya is seventeen years old. She is very intelligent. She has always been educated by private tutors here in this House because she suffers from a hereditary illness that makes it impossible, and undesirable, that she should leave the confines of the House and grounds.

'Secondly, because the Grand Duchess requires it, we – all of us here – live according to her wishes. What that means is simply that we dress, behave and live in a manner compatible with the era of her youth. For example, though we have electricity here, it is not in use. We have oil lamps, candles, coal fires. There are no televisions and no radios. You would be required to conform to these rules. As the Princess's tutor, you will be responsible for her study of the English language, but also for more general education related to those studies.

'You will be considered as a valued member of the household and not as domestic staff. You will eat here in this room with me or, on rare occasions, in the great dining room with the Grand Duchess and her senior staff and companions – we have a doctor, a lawyer and a priest in attendance several days each week.

'I will show you your quarters in a moment. One thing I really need to explain to you is that, during the period of your contract – which is renewable – you will have a great deal of free time and you will have all the facilities of the House at your disposal, but you are requested *not* to leave – that is, *not* to go outside the confines of these grounds.'

She paused to allow the seriousness of this piece of information to sink in.

'You will find us odd at first, Nicholas – I may call you that?'

I nodded.

'We live in a rather quaint, old-fashioned way, but it has its merits when you get used to it. Your salary will be saved for you and paid as a lump sum when your contract terminates.' She looked up at me. 'I do hope you accept, Nicholas; it really is a unique opportunity to meet some interesting people and live a different lifestyle for a while. The Princess Natalya is an exceptional person. She bears her illness bravely. Do you have any questions for me, Nicholas?'

Again, that warm smile.

'Er, yes, actually, Anya. You said "Princess"?'

'Yes. She is the Grand Duchess's niece and she has royal rank – you know, from Russia.'

I took that in slowly and then asked the obvious question. 'The illness that prevents the Princess from leaving the House – what is it, exactly?'

The answer was immediate. 'Oh, it's nothing you could catch, Nicholas. Really, it's not *that* sort of illness.'

I noticed the easy use now of my first name. 'So what sort of illness *is* it?' I persisted.

'Well, to be frank, no one seems to know exactly. It comes and goes. Sometimes she seems fine for weeks and then she's confined to her room for days on end…'

'I still don't quite understand…' I said, trying not to sound too obtuse.

Anya sighed. 'Well, it's a disorder of the mind…a sort of severe depression that overcomes her and changes her personality. Sometimes it's hard to know which symptoms are caused by the illness and which are caused by the treatment…which is sedation mainly, I believe. She's been seen by all sorts of specialists, professors, psychiatrists, and no one seems to know how to cure it. But it won't be a problem for you, Nicholas. We get a warning when it's about to happen and then Dr Voikin looks after her. Now, let me show you your quarters before you finally decide.'

She led me back to the great entrance hall and up the grand, red-carpeted stairs on the left side of the horseshoe and then along a wide passage to a door on the left. 'The whole of the left wing on this first floor is yours. It includes this schoolroom.' She pointed into a large room overlooking the front grounds of the House. 'And this is your sitting room.' We crossed an adjoining room, with a sofa and corner fireplace. 'And this is your bedroom.' We entered another small room with a double bed and wardrobe. I noticed a jug and ewer on a stand and a small bedside table with a candlestick. 'You see, Nicholas, it's self-contained, as they say. This door connects with the sitting room and then the schoolroom, and this door is to the main passageway; the bathroom is just across the corridor.'

During this monologue, I made general noises of approval, all the while thinking it a far cry from sleeping on the floor at Bruno's.

Anya seemed to be getting more animated and enthusiastic as we went along. 'Now,' she said archly, 'I'll introduce you to the staff.'

Leaving the bedroom by the corridor door, she led me to a dark-painted door right at the end of the passage. Here, at the back of the House, the narrow, winding stairs were uncarpeted and the painted walls a dirty cream. Carefully we descended, first to the ground-floor landing, and then a further four or five steps to a sort of semi-basement. It was a huge, stone-flagged room lit only above head height by ground-level windows and a big fire in a sort of walk-in stone fireplace.

At the window side, facing the back garden, were cookers and a great sink with slate worktops and, behind them, walls hung with copper kitchen utensils. Opposite, the fireplace had a few battered leather armchairs and a huge, scrubbed wooden table with benches either side.

Gathered in the middle of this room were the 'staff' in whose company I was about to spend several months of my life.

# CHAPTER 3

# Introductions, and the Veiled Lady

*'The world of reality has its limits; the world of imagination is boundless.'*

JEAN-JACQUES ROUSSEAU

' Madame Amélie, this is Nicholas, our new tutor.'

A short, heavily built middle-aged woman stepped forward, wiping her hands on her apron. She shook hands with me, staring intently with tiny black eyes set in a broad red face. There was something incredibly porcine about this Amélie, and she could only ever have been a cook, in this life.

Behind her, eyes downcast, was a young girl with frizzy blonde hair, wearing a black uniform over a high-collared white blouse.

'This is Agnès, our parlourmaid.'

Anya pulled her forward and she shyly shook hands without looking up.

Lastly, it was the turn of the tall, gaunt man who had admitted me earlier.

'This is Monsieur Serge, or Sergei Alexandrovitch.'

She smiled at him. He leaned forward and extended a hand towards me, and again I caught that whiff of saddle soap and tobacco.

'Serge is our chauffeur and handyman.'

'Groom and steward!' he corrected in a gruff voice, looking at Anya angrily. His handshake was stiff and strong, conveying, as he no doubt intended, the idea that *he* was the man of the house.

After all this excitement, each went back to his or her duties. Serge flopped in the old leather chair nearest the fire and began to roll a cigarette using Balkan Sobranie and liquorice paper. Agnès busied herself with the dishes. Only Amélie and Anya remained with me.

'He looks half-starved,' Amélie said to Anya as though I weren't present. 'He needs some decent Russian grub,' she added in her coarse French. 'Don't worry, Monsieur Nicholas, I'll look after you, fatten you up. You'll see.'

Anya smiled and guided me out. 'They're nice people once you get to know them. Now, Nicholas, go and fetch your belongings and come back as soon as you can. You won't change your mind, now, will you?'

She looked up and I felt that she was almost imploring me. I reassured her and told my first lie: I said that I was staying locally and would be only a short while.

Once I'd retrieved my suitcase from the café, I sat down on a bench and listened to the roar of the Paris rush-hour traffic on the nearby boulevard for about an hour and then returned to the House, suitcase in hand. There was a look of relief in Anya's eyes as she led me upstairs and left me in my room, with instructions to wear the new suit that I would find in the wardrobe and meet her for dinner downstairs in the library.

Never before had I possessed such a beautiful suit: dark grey, double-breasted, hand-made worsted. It fitted me absolutely perfectly, as did the white silk shirt, which felt wonderful against my skin. Even black leather brogues had been provided, and a selection of dark, tasteful silk ties. I had almost forgotten how to knot a tie.

I sat on the bed – *my* bed – and waited impatiently for the time to pass until dinner. Anya had made a positive impression on me. It was almost like meeting a sister I hadn't known existed. Less than eight hours earlier, I'd been sitting in a squalid café, penniless, without papers or a job and nowhere to sleep, talking about revolution; little better than a tramp. Now I was Monsieur Nicholas, tutor to a princess, staying in my own suite of rooms and wearing a hand-cut suit, new shoes and a silk shirt and tie! The total unpredictability of my life took my breath away.

To pass more time, I tinkered with the oil lamps so that I would know how to use them when it got dark. A few minutes before 8 p.m. I left my rooms by the passage door and, feeling rather self-conscious in my new clothes, made my way towards the huge horseshoe of the double stairways. From the landing of the double-height first floor, the main hall and entrance lay below in front of me, the black and white floor tiles sweeping up to the heavy crimson curtains now concealing the huge stained glass windows. The soft glow of the numerous oil lamps and the smell of the lamp oil pervaded the House.

As I descended slowly, taking in the splendour, the front doors opened and a woman swept hurriedly into the hall. As she turned to close the doors, I saw that she was wearing a long, dark, Edwardian-style dress with matching elbow-length gloves and an old-fashioned wide-brimmed hat of the sort that I always associate with the aristocracy at weddings. She turned and began to climb the stairway opposite to mine. We reached a point where I, descending, and she, ascending, were parallel, and she looked across at me. It was only then that I noticed that her face was completely hidden by a dark veil. I expected her to speak but, when she did not, I muttered a hesitant, '*Bonsoir, madame,*' not thinking until afterwards that I should perhaps have used a more elevated form of address. She did not reply and, reaching the central landing, walked off down the passage leading to the right wing of the House.

The library was bright and welcoming, at least the area near the fire where Anya was sitting, formally dressed, at a table for two.

'Good evening, Nicholas,' she greeted me in French. So far she had not asked me about my knowledge of Russian, and I certainly did not want to encourage any enquiry.

I sat down opposite her, feeling strangely shy in the rather intimate setting. She was too busy with the samovar to notice and soon broke the tension by swearing softly as she accidentally touched a finger to the hot metal. Eventually, she succeeded in providing me with a glass of hot, sweet, milkless tea which tasted better than it looked.

Agnès served dinner and we ate well. In fact, compared to my recent poverty-imposed diet, we ate better than I had eaten for months. There was wine and coffee and, of course, glass after glass of tea. I was ravenous but tried not to show it, as Anya was eating slowly and wanting to use the time to give me more information about the House and my rôle in its workings. Finally, during a pause, I remembered to ask her about the strange veiled lady I'd seen on the stairs.

Anya's smile disappeared for a moment and she looked at me straight in the eyes, her face very serious. 'That, Nicholas, was Madame Lili.'

'Madame Lili,' I repeated mechanically, pleased that at least my unanswered greeting had been correct.

Anya seemed to think that the mere utterance of the name explained everything, and fell silent.

'So?' I asked. 'Who is Madame Lili and what does she do here?'

Anya remained serious. 'She is the Grand Duchess's companion and her spiritual guide.'

'"Spiritual guide?" Aren't they supposed to be Red Indians…?' I repeated, unable to keep the hint of amusement out of my voice.

Anya didn't laugh. She didn't even smile, and I knew that I'd made my first gaffe. While I searched about for some way of redeeming myself, she remained silent and thoughtful. Suddenly she put her hand on my arm.

'Nicholas, we are the same age and we are both, in a way, strangers in this House. I hope that we can be friends and support each other so I feel I must warn you. Do not do anything to upset Madame Lili. Not only does she have the ear of the Grand Duchess, but she is a very, *very* dangerous woman.'

'Dangerous? How?'

'She has powers – don't ask me to explain, I can't – but she is capable of much harm. Please believe me.'

Her absolute seriousness impressed me and I mumbled some sort of reassuring remark.

Things went a bit quiet for a time but, after Agnès had cleared away, Anya suggested that we go to the kitchen. There, it was even more cheerful than the cosy library. Sergei sat next to the huge open fire, smoking some foul-smelling Russian tobacco, and Amélie sat opposite, still wearing her cook's apron, her huge face flushed even redder by the fire. Anya and I sat down on the benches and listened as Sergei recalled tales of his time as a Cossack with the White Army. His French was slow and heavily accented, adding to the atmosphere created by his words. It wasn't until much later, when I found out his age, that I realised that he could have been no more than a child during the Russian Civil War.

As the evening progressed, more tea was served and I had trouble keeping my eyes open. Eventually, Anya noticed this and told me gently that perhaps I needed to try out my new bedroom, an idea that I accepted gratefully.

I felt a strange light-headedness as I mounted the back stairs, almost as though I had had a lot to drink. Putting this down to the fumes from Sergei's cigarettes and pipe, I collapsed into bed and slept soundly for the first time in weeks, waking only when Agnès tapped on the door the next day with yet more tea and a pitcher of hot water for the washbasin. I felt slightly hungover, but the curiosity of meeting my seventeen-year-old royal student livened me up. And so, much greater was my disappointment when I was told that she was unwell.

With nothing to do all day, I turned to my own studies, broken by periods of exploration of the great old House.

The tall window of the schoolroom overlooked the front drive and was furnished only with a blackboard, bookshelves, a few armchairs and a couple of tables. The best room of my suite was certainly the little sitting room between the schoolroom and my bedroom. Although it was May, Agnès still lit fires and, sitting in a leather armchair reading Bergson, I felt as at home as anywhere I'd ever lived.

It took only a few minutes to lay out my possessions on the bed, and as I put my alarm clock on the bedside table I was amused to find a candlestick and matches, in addition to the main oil lamp hanging from the ceiling on a weighted pulley.

Having nothing further to do to complete my moving in, I set to exploring my new domain. My first discovery was a real surprise: one of the large cupboards in the schoolroom was actually the entrance to a narrow spiral stairway, and when I followed it down, groping in the dark, I came out via a wooden panelled door in the library, on to a sort of mezzanine floor where the top shelves of books could be reached from a narrow landing. Forward from here, another spiral stairway, this time wrought iron, continued to the floor. The entrance to the first stairway from the schoolroom was concealed on the library side by a hinged bookcase so, in effect, I had my own 'secret passage' to the library! I could tell from the copious cobwebs that no one had passed that way in a very long time. Anya had certainly not mentioned it, and I wondered whether she actually knew about it.

After that, things seemed a bit disappointing. The hallways of the House were rather grand, wide, carpeted and hung with a dark red embossed paper and, here and there, a pool of light cast by oil lamps on wall brackets, their soft yellow glow adding warmth and a distinctive smell to the heavy Victorian atmosphere.

The House seemed very quiet, with few comings and goings. Noises from other parts of the building seemed lost and muffled by the thick carpets and heavy drapes and, anyway, I soon realised that I was virtually alone on this side of the House, all the main living and sleeping quarters being in the right wing, separated from me by the cross-landing and another long passageway similar to mine and running parallel to it.

I decided that I should at least look busy, and went down to the library to sort through the books. After a while, Anya came in, smiling as usual, and seemed to be as pleased to see me there as I was to see her. She guided me round to the sitting area by the fire and lit the spirit burner under the samovar. My heart sank when I realised that the endless rounds of tea-drinking were about to recommence. While we were waiting, Anya presented me with several large books, old and musty, that contained, for the most part, black and white photographs taken during the Russian Civil War, 1917 to 1923. Bearded generals in Cossack hats leapt from the pages but I was relieved to see that the printed texts were in French or English and not in Cyrillic script.

'The Princess has to be knowledgeable on Russian history and it might be as well if you brushed up on it too.'

'Brushed up?' I repeated out loud, thinking that I knew virtually nothing about Russia or Russians, White or Red, except for a few émigrés I'd met here in Paris.

'Nicholas,' Anya said, looking very serious. 'You must understand that this House exists totally in that era. The Grand Duchess will speak to you – when you eventually meet her – about Bolshevism, White Russians, the fighting in the Crimea and the evacuation of the aristocracy, just as if it's happening now. You really have to understand that, or you will feel lost for the whole of your stay. You must open your mind to us and accept our rather odd way of living. That way, it will be so much more enjoyable for you.'

She leaned towards me, looking round as though she were part of a conspiracy, and lowered her voice to a whisper.

'They are living a dream here, Nicholas, and we must go along with it. Accept what you are told even if it seems ludicrous to you. Just play along…it's not so hard. It's like a chance to go back in time. Just accept that life here is like a theatrical play and you are playing a part. You do understand, don't you?'

She looked at me imploringly. Struck by her seriousness, I hastened to reassure her and had a sudden urge to put my cards on the table and tell her how my desperate situation had brought me here; but, although I felt a sort of bond with her, I couldn't bring myself to open up to her so soon.

As we sat looking at each other in silence, the door opened suddenly, startling us both. In the doorway, poised dramatically, stood a tall, slim woman wearing a big hat with a dark veil – the woman I had seen on the stairs the night before.

'Madame Lili! You startled us!' Anya exclaimed.

Madame Lili removed her hat and veil and turned towards us. Even by the dim light of the fire, she took my breath away!

The immediate impression was of an aristocratic face, with high cheekbones, delicate and well-shaped, and a fine, straight nose above full lips and mouth. Her dark brown hair was thick and shiny and piled on top of her head in a style I associated with the women in Victorian photographs.

Looking straight into my eyes, unblinking, she approached the table. I struggled to rise and meet her penetrating gaze. As she came closer, I was aware of a certain freshness emanating from her, newly arrived from the spring afternoon outside, but it was soon overpowered by the scent of violets, a heavy perfume that pervaded the air around me. She dazzled me. The cosy room was alive with her presence. I was drawn by her fixed, unwavering stare, and only vaguely aware that Anya was making an introduction.

'Madame Lili – Nicholas…our new tutor.'

The beautiful creature in front of me bowed her head slightly and extended her gloved hand in such a way that I was uncertain whether to shake it or kiss it. Finally, I just grasped it gently. Madame Lili was smiling at me now, her face very close to mine, her full mouth revealing perfect white teeth.

A feeling of intimidation swept over me and I could feel myself blushing at the embarrassment of her closeness. She must have seen this and moved even closer. Clasping my other hand, she held me tightly, pulling me down as she sat beside me, her face even closer to mine and her eyes boring into my very soul. This deliberate violation of my personal space intimidated me, and her stare became almost a physical contact.

Unable to hold her gaze any longer, I looked down, aware that I was blushing uncontrollably. Her hands continued to grip mine tightly and I noticed that her gloves were damp, although it was not raining outside.

'Thank you, Anya.' Her voice was deep yet soft. 'So, Monsieur Nicholas, tell me all about yourself, but first, what is your father's name?'

The question seemed odd; I couldn't see the relevance but answered mechanically, 'Frederick.'

'Ah ha! Feodor, in Russian. Good. I shall call you Nicolai Feodorovitch.'

Anya was later to explain the Russian fondness for patronymics.

'We will be friends, won't we, Nicolai Feodorovitch? And I will look after your spiritual guidance. I feel already that you are a lost soul, and that fate has brought you to this House, and to us. We will save you.'

Lacking any obvious verbal response, I managed a solemn nod of the head.

'Let me look at you, Nicolai; there is so much to see in you…'

She moved back from me but retained both my hands in hers, squeezing them tightly in her damp gloves. Her eyes were closed now, as if in a trance, the silence lasting for several moments.

Suddenly, she opened her eyes very wide and startled me. The irises were almost violet. A sort of dizziness was creeping up on me and I felt light-headed and not quite in control of myself. The room shimmered slightly and colours seemed to be brighter and deeper than before. Madame Lili's face seemed to fill my view – dark hair, dark red lips, white teeth and again that deep purple of her eyes. I began to feel uneasy, trapped and suffocated, and finally moved to pull my hands away.

Surprisingly, Madame Lili let go of my fingers immediately and withdrew to a normal distance. She stood up abruptly.

'Good afternoon, Nicholas. We will meet again soon. You will understand how much I can help you.'

And, with those enigmatic words, she was gone.

Anya's face now appeared in front of me. 'Nicholas! Nicholas! Are you all right?'

She seemed anxious and was tapping my face lightly. I made an effort to pull myself together and accepted a glass of water from her in the hope that it would make me feel better, then a glass of tea. A few minutes later and I was fighting to keep awake. I vaguely remember Anya helping me climb the stairs to my room. I fell asleep immediately, but strange dreams intruded and disturbed my mind. I had no defences.

# Chapter 4

# Listen to My Voice...

I awoke fully clothed, sprawled across the bed. I had missed dinner and slept right through the night. My head ached and I was shaking slightly – all the symptoms of a major hangover.

Mercifully, my appearance in the kitchen caused little comment. I managed a piece of toast and several cups of coffee, then decided that it was a good time to get some fresh air and explore the gardens.

The park around the House was not particularly big – land was at a premium in the Paris suburbs – but it was very secluded and divided up into separate areas by large clumps of shrubs. Just outside the back door, a café-sized table and chairs nestled in a small courtyard surrounded by lime trees and roses. Further down, a brick path led to a secluded arbour with a bench seat and, beyond that, a wide lawn dotted with clumps of rhododendrons just coming into flower.

I flopped down on the bench in the rose arbour, inhaling the spring air deeply to try to clear my head. Quite what had happened to me the afternoon before was a mystery. My first meeting with Madame Lili had left me weak and confused. Perhaps, in future, I should avoid too many cups of Russian tea! Vague glimpses of weird dreams came gradually into my mind and my head ached as never before.

As I opened my eyes slowly, squinting in the sunlight and looking out across the grass towards the property next door, a sudden movement caught my eye. Looking again, I saw a group of people in the distance, moving along the boundary. I could just make out that one woman was in an old-fashioned bath chair. Pushing her was a small man with a moustache and short beard, and next to him was a boy in a sailor suit. Behind this group were three young women, all in long, old-fashioned dresses. It wasn't, however, the Edwardian clothes that caught my attention but rather the fact that they all appeared as black and white, in monochrome against a colourful garden background – all, that is, except a fourth girl. Tall and very slim, dressed in a long, pale blue summer dress, hair piled on top of her head, she appeared in full colour, albeit subdued by the pastel shade of her dress and its edging of darker blue lace. This very odd phenomenon would have registered more with me if I had not felt so washed out. As it was, I closed my aching eyes for a moment and when I looked up the group had vanished, except for the fourth girl. She turned and raised her hand to me in a sort of wave. I got to my feet but, when I looked again, she too had vanished. It occurred to me that they must be neighbours and had returned to their home through a gap in the hedge that I could not see.

On returning towards the kitchen, I found Anya sitting at the café table, and she motioned for me to join her.

'Nicholas, I've been looking for you. God! You look awful; are you ill?'

'I don't know. Did I do something stupid last night?'

Anya looked at me, trying not to smile. 'No, Nicholas, you were fine. You just happened to meet Madame Lili at her most mischievous.'

'Mischievous? What does that mean?'

Anya bit her lip and then looked up at me. 'Nicholas, do you remember that I told you that Madame Lili is a very dangerous woman? You have now seen why. She has "the gift", and she can make strange and frightening things happen. Treat her with great respect.'

'"The gift?" Come on, Anya, you don't believe in all that mumbo-jumbo, do you?'

'Stop it! Just because you don't believe in it, it doesn't mean you're safe. Madame Lili is a gifted medium. You would do well not to upset her…that's all I'm saying. Now come with me. Put your other suit on, the dark blue one. I'm going to introduce you to the Princess.'

We went up to my apartment and Anya waited in the schoolroom while I changed my clothes. She looked me over when I rejoined her, straightened my tie, and then went off to find my pupil. I had determined to make a good start with the Princess Natalya: my relationship with her would affect the whole situation of my three-month stay in the House.

Nothing, however, had prepared me for her appearance that fine spring day. Anya entered first and stood back to admit 'Her Imperial Highness, Natalya Alexandrovna Romanova'. Framed by the doorway was a tall, slim girl, blonde hair pulled back in a formal bun. She wore a long, plain white dress with no jewellery or adornment whatsoever. But the thing that impressed me most was her extreme pallor. Her delicate face with its high cheekbones was somehow reminiscent of Madame Lili except for its total lack of any colour, including her lips, which had only the slightest pink hue. Dark shadows encircled her blue-grey eyes and lent weight to her sad expression – a beautiful face that never smiled.

She moved slowly towards me as if each step was an effort, not taking her eyes from mine, and slowly lifted her hand.

Again not sure whether to shake it or kiss it, I did neither but instead managed a self-conscious clasping of her right hand with a simultaneous awkward inclination of my head – neither a bow nor a nod. She stood looking straight at me and I felt that, in spite of her obvious youth and frailty, she still managed to convey a sort of regal dignity.

To my relief, she did not speak to me, and I cursed myself for not asking Anya how I should address this striking young woman. While I hesitated, she took the initiative and almost smiled at me; her even white teeth somehow completing her pallor. The look, though, was warm enough. Anya excused herself with something approaching a curtsey and left me alone with my pupil. There followed a moment of awkwardness; neither of us seemed to know what to do next.

My overall impression was that I was dealing with an invalid, and so I pulled up the nearest chair. She sat down and looked up at me questioningly.

'Your Highness…' I heard myself saying.

'Natalie,' she corrected. It seemed a little informal but I had little choice but to comply.

'Er…Natalie…I hope I may be of service…' I mumbled, feeling strangely self-conscious in the face of her stare.

'Your name again?' she asked softly.

'Nicholas.'

'What do your friends call you, Nicholas?'

'Well, here in France, usually…Nico.'

She looked at me, very still, head on one side.

'Then I shall call you *Monsieur* Nicholas, because you are older than I and age demands respect.' Again, the white smile.

'But I should call you…'

'Natalie,' she insisted. 'When we are alone,' she added.

Her French seemed fluent enough. There was, of course, an accent, quite charming but oddly not Russian. Her intonation was more Germanic – as a Swiss German might speak French. I made a mental note to ask Anya about it. I'd noticed the same accent with Madame Lili's French. But then, I didn't suppose any of the family had lived in Russia since 1918!

Natalie's English also seemed quite fluent, and I was relieved that she wouldn't have to start as an absolute beginner.

We spent an hour together and to my delight I found her easy to talk to. Young as she was, she had that aristocratic ability to put people at their ease. Finally, very politely, she excused herself by saying that she was a little tired but looked forward to starting her studies in earnest the next day. I stood up as she rose and walked to the door before I could get there to open it. Turning, she smiled at me.

'Don't be late, Nico!'

After all the formality, it was a welcome, if childlike, comment, and I found myself smiling back.

Flopping down on my sofa, I breathed a long sigh of relief that the ice was broken. I thought of Bruno, Aurélie and Jean-Marie in the grubby café near the Boul'Mich. and decided, ungratefully, that I didn't miss them at all. I allowed myself a certain smugness at the sheer comfort of my new-found situation.

An hour was spent planning the next day's lessons and then, with a certain lightness of step, I skipped down the servants' back stairs to the kitchen in search of some lunch.

The afternoon passed quickly, talking to Anya and again leafing through the old books about the Russian Civil War that she had insisted I read. Soon it was time for dinner. Instead of eating together in the library, Anya suggested we join the staff in the kitchen.

Once dinner had been served 'upstairs', everyone seemed to relax and, after it had been cleared away, it was our turn and we sat down on the benches at the long scrubbed wooden table near the huge stone fireplace and ate a wonderful meal with Amélie, Sergei and Agnès. If the atmosphere seemed a little strained initially, the amusement of the others at my ignorance of Russian cuisine soon broke the ice. The enjoyable evening that followed was no doubt partly due to the bottle of vodka that Serge produced – yet another Russian custom to be introduced to me.

There followed a good night's sleep. Now that I had met my pupil, I felt more relaxed and, perhaps prematurely, overcome by a cosy feeling of belonging, almost as if I had found a family of sorts. Perhaps that's exaggerating a bit but I certainly experienced a sort of warm glow of security and continuity and considered the House, for all its oil lamps and dark wood panelling, a bright and cosy refuge from my recent sea of troubles.

The morning brought its own surprises. I made a special effort in washing, shaving and combing my unruly hair and trying to get used to wearing a tie again. I felt my new, beautifully tailored suits and silk shirts deserved it. Thankfully, I wasn't expected to wear a butterfly collar!

For some reason, I half expected Natalya to be late – after all, there was no one to tell her off – but she knocked on the school door promptly at 9 a.m. I had the lessons all planned out, and felt confident and ready for any eventuality.

Nothing, however, could have prepared me for my surprise at opening the door.

Natalya was standing back, partly obscured by the shadows of the gloomy passageway, but, as she stepped forward and entered the sunlit classroom, she took my breath away. Gone was the frumpy long cotton frock of the day before, the flat shoes and the pulled-back hair. In front of me, very conscious of the effect she was creating, stood a very beautiful young woman. An elegant, cream-coloured two-piece outfit hugged her slim figure, heeled shoes increased her already considerable height, a beautiful high-collared Victorian blouse enhanced her graceful neck, and an antique golden chain with a Russian Orthodox two-barred cross hung upon her chest.

She couldn't fail to notice my surprise. She turned to face me and moved closer. Subtle make-up hid the pallor of her face, and a hint of pink lip gloss emphasised the whiteness of her teeth. As she moved, a musky perfume reached me.

But her hair! I stared at the short blonde bob framing her face, cut diagonally away from her high cheekbones on one side and hanging like a gold curtain across her eye.

Like an idiot, I blurted out, 'You cut your long hair!'

To my relief, her reaction was merely to laugh.

'No, I didn't, Monsieur Nicholas…' she said, smiling and with a faintly mocking tone. 'I just took my hairpiece off!'

I continued to stare at her foolishly.

'Look', she explained, 'my aunt, the Grand Duchess, likes us all to dress and look like people from the times of her youth – you know, 1900 – long dresses, long hair, big hats, that sort of thing. But it's hard work having long hair, so we cheat. We wear hairpieces.'

She burst out laughing at my obvious bewilderment.

'What, all of you?' I asked, thinking of Anya.

'All of us, except Madame Lili and the Grand Duchess, of course.'

I tried to take it all in. Before me stood the most stunning-looking girl that I had ever seen, even in a city like Paris where beautiful women were numerous.

'Well? Are you going to ask me to sit down, *monsieur*?'

'Of course, *mademoiselle*,' I mumbled, trying to recover some of the dignity of my office.

She sat in front of me, crossing her legs, the girl giving place to a sophisticated young woman evidently pleased to have had such an obvious effect on me.

'Er, well, yes…I'd thought we would start by you giving me an idea of the extent of your spoken English. Would you just read the paragraph I've marked in this book?'

Serious now, she read slowly and clearly, with an impressive grasp of the pronunciation of the language. Again I was surprised by her intonation, which was definitely more German-sounding than Russian – the same accent that could be heard in her French.

As the lesson wore on, Natalie seemed to be trying hard to please me. Her slightly 'diva'-ish debut was soon replaced by a serious, even prim attention to the niceties of social etiquette, and by the time we stopped for lunch she was every bit the regal princess again.

When, after lunch, I received a message that 'the Princess regrets…she will not be able to attend further today' from Anya, I had to admit to feeling very disappointed. The change in Natalya since the previous day had so much confused me that I found myself confiding in Anya about it when we took tea together in the library.

She listened to me, serious, with her head on one side as if concentrating on everything I was saying. Eventually, after a long silence, she put her hand on my arm.

'Nicholas, it is a symptom of the Princess's illness that she has mood swings, between elation and depression. You know, she bears a great responsibility in that she is one of the few last immediate descendants of the Tsar of all the Russias…'

She stopped speaking to look at me and, when I didn't answer, continued, 'She is seventeen years old, with all the difficulties that age brings. She is on the verge of womanhood, a difficult enough time without having a depressive illness to contend with.'

She remained looking at me, inviting a reply.

'What are you trying to tell me, Anya?'

'I'm not *trying* to tell you anything! I'm sure you understand!' Her irritation sounded in her voice. 'You are almost twenty-three years old, Nicholas. That's maturity, when a girl is seventeen! You have lived in the modern world, outside, in a big cosmopolitan city like Paris. Perhaps you have lived in London too, I don't know...but Natalie...she knows only this House and the people in it. She is, in every respect, an innocent, very vulnerable, and I worry about her.'

'She's safe with me.'

'Is she, Nicholas? Is she, really?'

'Is that some sort of a warning, Anya?'

'Do I *have* to give you a warning, Nicholas?'

She smiled then, to lighten the atmosphere and then continued, softly, 'Well, there might be times...there might be occasions when Natalie's behaviour may not quite come up to appropriate standards for someone of her rank and obligations. That is...' She was getting flustered. 'Oh, that is, you may need to employ some decorum – diplomacy – of your own from time to time. Now, let's drop it, shall we? Natalie is officially in the hands of Madame Lili, her chaperone and spiritual mentor...'

Her voice trailed off when, as if by some strange coincidence, Madame Lili appeared in the doorway, her heavy perfume instantly filling the room.

She stretched a gloved hand towards me in such a way this time that I was obviously meant to kiss it. I managed a self-conscious touch of the lips against the black satin material, and felt her huge dark eyes boring into me.

'Nicolai Feodorovitch...' she greeted me, using the patronymic. 'The Princess has conveyed to me her pleasure at her first studies with you; a good start!'

Not sure what to reply, I nodded politely at the compliment. She looked past me. 'My dear Anya Pavlova! I am so pleased to find you here too. I wish to ask a service of you both...'

Her deep voice made her French sound very pleasant. 'I am expecting some guests this evening. We shall need this room. There is a conference…I fear the war is not going well for the White Army. You do understand, don't you both?'

I understood only that we were being asked to leave.

'What war?' I asked Anya as we walked down towards the kitchen.

'The Civil War in Russia, silly!' she laughed.

'But that ended in 1923.'

She stopped, turned to me and winked. 'Nicholas, remember what I told you. This is a strange House and we are strange people. Try not to concern yourself about it.'

We ate well with the staff but somehow the cosy, convivial atmosphere of the previous evening was not recreated.

I found myself upstairs, alone in the schoolroom, still early in the evening. It was a fine spring night but quite dark, and the view from the open front windows did not even extend to the gravel drive below. High on the horizon was the amber glow from the streetlights of Paris and, here and there, a glimpse of yellow headlights, and red rear lights, and just audible was a faint rumble from the traffic. Heavy cloud blotted out the moon and stars. Paris was near, but fifty years away.

Suddenly, the silence of the evening was broken by what sounded like horses approaching. Still nothing was visible from the window, but the sound of hooves on the gravel became louder and louder, finally ceasing, apparently at the front doors below.

Curiosity got the better of me and I crept along the corridor towards the stair head, from where I could see the front doors; I was just in time to see the closing of the library door. Disappointed, and with nothing particular to do, I fell to wondering whom Madame Lili might be entertaining in the library.

It was as I resumed my aimless wandering around the school room that I remembered the 'secret' stairs in the cupboard and, with a recklessness that later surprised me, I decided to creep down and take a look. What possessed me to do such a thing, I don't know. My only excuse is that I was feeling rather light-headed and wondered later if Serge had added anything to the several glasses of Russian tea that he had given me after dinner.

Whatever the reason, I crept down the narrow, dusty, winding stairs and very gingerly eased open the small door in the section of bookshelf running round the mezzanine balcony of the library.

As the gap widened, I could hear the murmur of voices speaking in Russian, slowly and solemnly. A bit further and I was out on to the narrow landing that gave access to the very top bookshelves. I moved stealthily along to where I could look down into the room while still being hidden from view by the iron spiral staircase. Very cautiously, I lifted my head above the stair rails.

Below me was the oddest scene.

Standing around the long book table, poring over a map, were three soldiers in dark uniforms. One – who, because he stood between the two others, I took to be the leader – was short and heavily built. He had a grey beard and moustache, and the hair that escaped from his fur hat was white and unkempt. To his right stood a much smarter soldierly man in a military overcoat and peaked cap. But the weirdest of the three was certainly the man to the leader's left.

He was tall, unnaturally so, perhaps well over two metres, and this height was emphasised by both his extreme thinness and his strange, almost comical uniform. He wore a three-quarter-length coat pulled in tight at the waist by a wide leather belt holding a large curved knife, and, below, high black riding boots. His long, gaunt face ended in a goatee beard with a large black moustache. His long frame was topped off by a tall astrakhan Cossack hat.

All three were clearly outlined by the shaded oil lamp that hung over the reading table. But there was something wrong with the picture that I didn't take in until later when I went over the scene in my mind – just as with the people I had seen in the garden yesterday, they were grey, black and white! The whole scene was monochrome.

Suddenly, a movement in the shadows behind the man caught my eye. To my dismay, Madame Lili appeared in the circle of the lamplight and looked immediately up at me; that is, she looked up straight in my direction. There was no way she could have seen me, hidden as I was by the spiral stairs, but she knew, somehow, that I was there. I was sure of it, and even more sure about the anger on her beautiful face.

Under the glare of her gaze, I shrank back further into the shadows and retreated furtively to the door in the bookcase, silently closing it behind me and creeping quickly up the stairs to the schoolroom cupboard. Back in my room, when I thought it all through, I tried to convince myself that she could not have seen me after all, and went to bed cursing my stupidity in laying myself open to such embarrassment.

By morning, I had managed to put this rather trivial incident to the back of my mind and was looking forward to seeing the Princess again.

She duly appeared right on time, dressed as before and this time wearing a heavy perfume reminiscent of Madame Lili's, so heavy and strong that it was almost overpowering. On this occasion, she seemed less eager to study than before, and she appeared more relaxed, more 'natural', and not trying to impress me with a maturity which she did not yet possess. She smiled a lot, showing her pretty white teeth, and dutifully laughed at my attempts at wit. When she did that, there was something vaguely reminiscent of Madame Lili, and I wondered if they had common ancestry: both were tall and slim, both spoke French with a soft but unmistakable German accent, and both had a sort of 'regal' or aristocratic presence.

The day passed too quickly for me. I surprised myself by finding great enjoyment in teaching English and at the same time enjoying the company of a very lovely young lady, unspoiled by big city ways.

For her part, Natalie behaved in such a relaxed way that it was hard to believe that she could suffer from any sort of psychosis. It would be very wrong to suggest she flirted with me or behaved in any way inappropriate for a pupil/master relationship.

Here and there, I learned more about the people and layout of the House. Her Imperial Highness the Grand Duchess was very old and kept to her suite of rooms on the third floor, served by the right-hand staircase and corridor. Nearby, her companion and spiritual advisor, Madame Lili, had her own sitting room and bedroom. On the ground floor was a large room that served as the main dining room and was also used for occasional soirées and Madame Lili's séances.

There was also a surgery with a small day-bed used by Dr Voikin on the occasions when Natalya was very ill and he needed to stay over. Natalya herself had a modest bedroom next door. Both she and Madame Lili ate with the Grand Duchess, as did Anya from time to time. This last information surprised me a little, as I had come to see Anya very much as 'staff'. As the Grand Duchess's secretary and housekeeper, though, she seemed to play an ambivalent role, with a foot in both camps. Before we parted, Natalya reminded me that I also would receive the occasional summons to attend dinner with the Grand Duchess – not something I felt I could look forward to experiencing.

Natalie's departure, after our several hours together, brought a pang of loneliness and I was pleased to go down to the kitchen for dinner.

There followed another of those cosy, happy evenings with people I was already beginning to look upon as a new family. Again Amélie produced a superb meal and we ate and drank, as before, seated on the benches along the scrubbed table in front of the fire. Serge insisted on vodka interspersed with glasses of hot, sweet Russian tea. In spite of the food inside me, it wasn't long before I began to feel a bit light-headed, and this wasn't helped by the clouds of heavy Russian tobacco smoke thrown out by Serge's pipe as he prepared to regale us with one of his tall stories.

To my surprise, this happy atmosphere was suddenly interrupted by Anya who, after being called away, returned looking serious. She leaned over me from behind and whispered in my ear, 'Madame Lili wishes to speak to you, Nicholas, in the library.'

'What, now? Can't it wait until tomorrow?'

'Yes, now! She insisted upon it. She seems very upset. You must go immediately. Do *not* keep her waiting.'

I looked up at Anya, suspecting a joke and expecting to see her smiling. But she was deadly serious and obviously troubled. Reluctantly I stood up, her uneasiness communicating itself to me, and stifling the smart remark that had come to mind. Making suitable excuses, I followed her out of the kitchen and down the long wide passage towards the front of the House.

'What's it about, Anya? Did I do something wrong?'

'I don't know. But it's not a good idea to upset Madame Lili. She...' Her voice trailed off. She hustled me along faster, stopped outside the library door and, when I hesitated, thrust me forward and whispered fiercely, 'Be careful, Nico!'

And I was into the room.

All the main lights were out. Only a solitary oil lamp and the flickering red light of the fire lit the room. On one of the two small chairs around the table sat Madame Lili. She did not rise as I moved cautiously towards her, uneasy then, for the first time. Her perfume hit me like a wall of fragrance.

'Nicolai Feodorovitch,' she said in a low voice.

There was no warmth in the greeting. I found myself in front of her, trying to pull my wits together and shake off the lethargy that risked overcoming me. I took her outstretched hand; her glove felt damp. I realised that I was meant to kiss her hand, not shake it, and I bent my head to do so. She looked up so suddenly that it startled me.

I will never forget that look. Her eyes seemed almost black, the pupils filling the violet of her irises, and they penetrated my brain with almost physical force. Instinctively, I drew back. A tremor, starting in my bowels, ran up my spine, and I shuddered violently, vaguely aware that her sensual lips were open in a cynical smile, the big white teeth parted slightly. But I could not lift my eyes from that cold unblinking stare.

My knees started to buckle under me and somewhere, far away now, her voice was ordering me to sit down.

We faced each other then, across the small table. She was holding both my wrists tightly, so very tightly that it began to hurt. I could not speak to protest, and the odd feeling of detachment increased all the time. And still her eyes held mine and I could not look away.

'Why were you spying on me, Nicolai Feodorovitch, last night, in the library?' She hissed the question.

I tried to answer but my mouth had gone dry.

'I…I wasn't spying, Madame Lili,' I finally managed to blurt out.

She seemed not to hear, and continued, 'Do you not understand how terrible this war is? We Whites against that filthy Bolshevik scum – the anti-Christ dregs of Russia…'

She seemed to be talking for her own benefit; I didn't know how I was expected to answer and was more concerned about my growing physical unease.

'I…er…don't understand, Madame Lili. Please…I wasn't spying on you…it was just my curiosity…it got the better of me…'

I knew it sounded like grovelling and I didn't care.

'*Curiosity*?' She spat the word. Then, as suddenly as it had erupted, her anger subsided. 'Have you ever been to Russia, Nicholas?' she murmured softly.

I shook my head, not trusting my voice.

'Do you know how vast it is? Can you imagine how cold it can be? Do you understand how savage this war is, Russian against Russian?'

No, I didn't know. Nor did I care; it had been over for forty-five years!

I tried to look away from her. A terrible uneasiness had gripped my mind and the awful feeling of detachment completely overcame me. The room, the fire, the lamplight, all seemed to be receding into the background as if I were seeing the room through the wrong end of a telescope. Giddiness hit me, and the colours around me kaleidoscoped. Realising that I really was ill, I tried to pull away, wanting to get to my feet, make some hurried excuse and leave. But Madame Lili intensified her grip on my wrists with extraordinary force and I felt the strength ebb from me.

'Look at me, Nicholas! Look at me! Now, listen to me, listen to me, listen to my voice…'

The room had gone cold and dim; only the vaguest outlines were discernible.

'Listen to me. Listen to my voice,' she said again, seemingly from a great distance.

For a moment, I felt I was floating, and then what was left of the room turned faster and faster and everything went white – a bright, dazzling white...

It was cold. It was very, very cold. It was cold like I had never known, and with the cold came a brilliant clarity that I had never before experienced. I saw everything as though the edges had been outlined by a black pen. The sky was black and the stars glittered like sparks. The snow stretched away around me, flat, monotonous, endless; the only horizon a dark fringe of pines miles away across that frozen waste.

The snorting of my horse brought me back from the emptiness of this awful place and my own mind.

Great clouds of steam emanated from the horse's nostrils, its ice-encrusted head turned towards me. Without any warning it crashed to the ground, pitching me head-first on to the smooth wind-driven snow. I staggered up, my long greatcoat heavy with powdered snow. The horse whinnied pitifully and rolled its great bloodshot eyes. It was dying, and my heart went out to it. I took off my mittens, dragged the heavy revolver from its stiff leather holster on my belt and held its muzzle against the horse's head. The shot was deafening. Its sharp report startled me and reverberated around the empty starlit waste like thunder.

Suddenly, fear gripped me. What if *they* had heard...they must be close behind... And even as I said this to myself I looked up and my stomach churned. There, on the horizon, a thin black line appeared and grew darker and wider even as I sought to focus on it. They were coming...!

Automatically, I started to run. The snow was knee-deep and slowed me down as in a nightmare. The trees, the dark trees...

but even as I turned towards them my heart was sinking. Those trees were mile upon mile away.

There was nowhere to run to, and nowhere to hide.

Now, the first of the riders was clearly visible; behind him a dark mass of galloping horses and men, snow flying off them like sea spray. The starlight glinted off their drawn sabres, and clouds of steam swirled about their horses.

At first, all was silence, then I fancied I could discern a rising, high-pitched yell that curdled my frozen blood and rooted me to the spot. I wanted to vomit but could not move, even for that. A strange shiver ran up my bowels and I felt a warm wetness soak my trousers and I knew that I was about to die.

Still I did not, could not, move. The blood was frozen in my veins and I prayed the cold would take me before my imminent execution.

Relentlessly, the yelping horde bore down on me, poor petrified creature that I was.

Suddenly, the awful waiting was over. They were there, all around me, steaming horses snorting and pawing the snow, breathing hard, the smell of their sweat increasing my nausea.

The leader rode a pace towards me. I had not moved and he, thinking that I had frozen to death, or died of fear, probably felt cheated. Eventually, I managed to look up at him...a cruel, gaunt face, young, so very young, the red star on his fur hat the only colour on his grey uniform, the greatcoat powdered with snow.

He did not speak. His horse, tense from the gallop, moved its head from side to side, snorting and jerking at the reins.

Without a word, the commissar began to raise his sabre, the frozen, polished steel gleaming in the clear starlight. It stayed, poised above his head, as if frozen there for all time. Then a blinding flash exploded against my head and I sank, gratefully, into blackness...

Someone was calling my name, distant at first but then loudly and insistently. A circle of light showed against the blackness, coming closer and closer and gradually resolving itself into the glowing shade of an oil lamp.

Images appeared. Madame Lili's face loomed up close to mine. She was tapping my cheek and shaking me.

'Nicholas! Nicholas!'

It was Anya's voice; she was holding my arm and calling softly. Slowly, very slowly, the room came into focus − the fire, the oil lamp, the small table. Madame Lili and Anya were holding me up, concern etched on their faces.

Voices, more voices, a deep voice. Strong, masculine arms gripped me...the familiar smell of leather and tobacco told me that Serge was there. Now Madame Lili's voice:

'Nicholas seems to have been taken ill...a malaise...help Anya to get him to his room. I will ask Dr Voikin to give him something to help him sleep.'

I was moving, climbing upstairs on legs of jelly, my weight supported by Serge and Anya; he silent, she whispering encouragement. Then I was on the bed, shaking, focusing on Anya, though Madame Lili's heavy perfume told me she was there too, and I could hear the voice of the doctor. A slight sting in my arm and then a feeling of wellbeing and calmness swept over me, bringing with it the oblivion of sleep.

The sun was well risen when I awoke and, believing that I would be late for Natalie's classes, I leapt out of bed, only to fall in a heap on the floor as my knees buckled! I started up, giddy and with my head pounding, and sat on the end of the bed. Slowly, my mind started to clear, and I rose and made it to the washstand and tipped the cold water from the ewer over my aching head.

My suit lay carefully folded on a chair and, never having possessed pyjamas, I was naked and shivering from the shock of the cold water. Glimpses of the evening before flitted across my mind, and I blushed at the realisation that whoever put me to bed must have undressed me.

I cut myself shaving, my hand still shook so much. Still only half awake, I began to worry. I had all the symptoms of a mighty hangover, but one glass of red wine at dinner and a couple of vodkas with Serge should not have produced that effect on me. Again, I wondered at the wisdom of drinking Russian tea.

The events of the evening were gradually coming together in my mind: the snowy, endless wasteland, the steely cold, the steaming horses and the violet starry sky edged with black firs… Instinctively my hand went to my face, half expecting to feel shattered bone and blood. Nothing. I shuddered again and gripped the bedrail, unable to move.

A gentle tapping at my door brought me back to reality – if, indeed, anything in this strange House could be called 'real'. Wrapping a towel around my waist, I opened the unlocked door. Anya stood in front of me and I saw her eyes widen as she took in my wild, semi-naked appearance. Anxiously, she looked down the hallway and whispered, 'You'd better let me in!'

In the room, she sat down on the bed, turned her eyes up to me and, for the second time, I noticed that one was brown and the other almost green. She managed a half-smile.

'Nicholas, do you feel as terrible as you look?'

'Worse! Christ, Anya, what the hell happened to me last night?' And without giving her a chance to reply, 'Did I do something really bad? Will they give me the sack? What about Natalya's lessons…?'

'Calm down, Nico!' I noticed the use of the endearment. 'It's Saturday.'

She stood up and suddenly touched my face where I had nicked it with the razor.

'Oh, you silly boy! What did I tell you when you first came here? Madame Lili is not just the Duchess's companion, she is her spiritual guide, and I also told you that she has the gift.'

'Yes, so you said! What, you mean, "second sight" and all that rubbish? That she's, what – a medium? Come on, Anya, this is 1968, not the Dark Ages...'

'Stop!' she cut me off abruptly, her finger against my lips. There was not a trace of amusement in her face. 'Stop, Nicholas! How can you ridicule what you don't understand? Especially after what she did to you last night!'

I made to speak but she held up her hand.

'I saw you, Nicholas. I helped put you to bed. You were absolutely terrified; so much so that we feared for your sanity.'

'We?' I asked.

'Serge and myself. Even Madame Lili seemed concerned. Listen to me now, Nicholas: she is very, very dangerous. Better to have her for a friend, even if it means compromising your secular beliefs. This is a strange House and you cannot fight it. You could be happy here but only if you open your mind and accept...accept even what you cannot understand. You have been too long around your precious Bergson, Sartre and Camus. Here is not the "Age of Reason". Here is the spiritual and the unknown. Accept us, and you will learn much – much that you will not find elsewhere.'

Not knowing how to answer this obviously well-intentioned sermon, I just nodded.

'Now finish dressing and come to the kitchen for coffee. Amélie will cook you something to perk you up.'

I opened the door for her, still holding the towel over my nakedness, and she turned and gave me a sisterly peck on the cheek before moving away towards the servants' stairs.

As I stood at the door watching her walk away, a slight movement from my right made me turn around, almost losing my towel in the process, and just in time to see Natalya dart from an alcove and disappear towards the other wing of the House.

*Great!* I thought. *Now she has seen her tutor half-naked! Can my day get any worse?*

I felt steadily better as the day wore on, did a bit of private study for my course and sat and leafed through the old photographs in the Russian history books that Anya had left for me. By dinnertime, seated round the table in the kitchen, I was back to normal and enjoying Amélie's Russian cuisine, while being careful to give Sergei's home-made vodka a miss. Anya left us for a moment and, when she returned, she drew me to one side.

'Nico, I have been mending fences for you. Madame Lili is currently in the library, alone. I think you would do well to make your peace with her. She believes you were spying on her the other night. Come along, use some diplomacy and that "boyish charm" and apologise, even if you think you didn't do anything wrong…please, for me, and the smooth running of the House.'

I couldn't refuse Anya. She had been so good to me. So, straightening my tie, I headed with some misgiving along the dimly lit corridor towards the front of the House. The oil lamps there spread a warm yellow glow and gave off considerable heat on that slightly chilly spring evening, and I was surprised at how quickly I had become used to their smell, which had been so noticeable when I first came to the House.

When I pushed open the library door after a couple of timorous knocks, Madame Lili had her back to me sitting at the small table.

'Good evening, Nicolai Feodorovitch,' she said, without turning round, as if somehow she had seen me come in.

'Good evening, Madame Lili,' I said hoarsely, my throat suddenly dry. She looked up at me as I walked around to face her, her long, dark hair drawn away from her face in a sort of ponytail, her lips parted against those big white teeth in a cold smile.

Suddenly, as she brought her dark eyes up to mine, I felt a frisson of fear run up my spine, and I tried to look away from her steady, penetrating gaze, telling myself not to be so stupid. She lifted her hand for me to kiss and it gave me an excuse to avoid those eyes. Her perfume seemed to hit me in waves and again, in spite of all my efforts, I began to feel light-headed.

'So nice to see you, Nicholas. We have been concerned – you seemed unwell last night. Some sort of malaise – a nightmare perhaps? Please do sit down.'

She smiled again. This time there seemed to be some warmth in it.

'Madame Lili...'

I hesitated, and she leaned forward and arched her eyebrows for me to continue.

'Madame Lili, I fear that I may have inadvertently upset you...the other night, here in the library, in the presence of your guests...'

I trotted out the formal little apology I had rehearsed coming down the passage. 'I didn't mean to spy on you, though I understand that that is how it must have appeared. It was thoughtless of me, and ill-mannered. I can only ask you to excuse my...er...lapse...'

For a long moment she said nothing but looked at me intently, as though trying to decide whether I was sincere. Then, having apparently made up her mind, she exclaimed, 'Bravo, Nicholas, elegantly put! I accept your handsome apology. Now, we will be friends. Would you like that, Nicolai?'

Her sudden warmth threw me a bit and I just nodded vigorously.

'Good. That's settled, then. You must, of course, now that we are friends again, come to one of my séances; I would be most hurt if you did not...'

And that was it. I'd dropped neatly into her trap! Now I was to join in with the mumbo-jumbo! Not, of course, that I gave any indication of my scepticism to Madame Lili. But Anya's words kept ringing in my ears: *You could be happy here but only if you open your mind and accept...accept even what you cannot understand.*

My thoughts refocused on the room and on Madame Lili. She seemed quite relaxed now, at her most charming. The spider had caught her fly. She flashed a heartwarming smile at me and I had to admit that she was indeed a very beautiful woman. Perhaps a séance or two with her might not be so bad...all that holding hands in the dark. And who knew, she might even conjure up my great-grandad so that I could ask him what happened to the family fortune!

But, in spite of my attempted flippancy, a little voice in my head was saying, *Careful, Nico, careful.*

After some more small talk and my polite refusal of the inevitable glass of tea from the samovar, we parted; friends now.

And I opted for an early night.

Once I was in my room, a great feeling of relief came over me, washing away the earlier anxiety. I told myself I had my own bed, my own room, with no financial worries and a full stomach. True, this was a strange house and my employers were unusual, eccentric people, but I felt secure here. I had seen Paris in all its beauty and, most recently, at its most violent and disturbed. I had been one step away from sleeping rough, perhaps even a stay in jail for vagrancy and passport offences and now...

I started to drift away, never imagining for one moment that my feeling of safety was entirely misplaced.

There was a movement. It was pitch black in the room and yet something had awakened me...a slight click, the sudden draught as the door opened? Yet it was locked.

I lay perfectly still, listening. The silence was absolute. And yet I knew something was there, standing in the darkness at the end of the bed.

It was obvious that there was no time to fumble for matches and light the candle that was placed somewhere on my bedside table. But I wanted to jump up, confront it and take the initiative, so to speak.

Yet I did nothing. Fear pinned me to the spot and, before I could attempt to overcome it, I saw a shadow rise over the bed. When I say 'saw', I mean only that the darkness there became darker still, in the vague outline of a figure.

My shout was just a groan that died in my throat as fear paralysed me; my heart was beating furiously and I struggled to breathe.

Then 'it' was upon me. It leapt at me from the foot of the bed. As in a nightmare, I fought to move leaden limbs and to articulate some sort of cry for help.

The seconds passed so slowly and still the thing was upon me, my arms pinned under the bedclothes by its weight. Suddenly my voice came back and I let out a bellow that ended in a piercing yell. At the same time, I felt a sharp stabbing pain in my upper arm as I freed it from the sheets.

We fought, I to escape and the thing to hold on to me. Somewhere in the depths of my subconscious I felt I knew my attacker, but this recognition was not communicated to my mind.

Voices sounded outside my room. The door burst open to reveal the light of an oil lamp and then the room seemed full of people. I recognised Anya and Serge and there was also a dapper, suited man who I had not seen before.

As the lamplight swept the bed, I saw with total amazement that my spectral assailant was…my pupil, Natalya!

Dressed in a shapeless nightshirt and deathly pale, she stared up at us, wild-eyed and crouching defensively. Without a word, Serge and the smaller man stepped forward and, with infinite gentleness, lifted the poor girl off my crumpled bed and carried her from the room. As they slowed to negotiate the door, Natalya looked back reproachfully at me and I saw her staring eyes were full of tears.

Suddenly all was quiet; everyone had gone except for Anya. It was only then that I realised that I had been stabbed. An empty syringe lay on the bed, its needle snapped off short. The other half was in my arm and just beginning to make itself known.

Anya tutted softly when she saw it and told me to sit down and find something to cover myself with while she went to Dr Voikin's surgery for some tweezers. Moments later, she returned and gently eased the long needle from deep in my upper arm. It hurt like hell but I tried not to show it. I did jump though when she dabbed it with iodine.

'Remember that Natalie is not well, Nicholas,' she said. 'She has occasional fits – symptomatic of her illness – but she isn't normally violent. I can only apologise on her behalf. It must have been very frightening for you. It will not happen again. Here...' She held out her hand with two small white tablets. 'Take these. Dr Voikin prescribed them to help you sleep. We'll discuss all this in the morning. All will be explained. Goodnight, Nico. Be sure to take them.'

She leaned forward and gently kissed me on the forehead.

## Chapter 5

# Jasmin de Corse, Tatianouchka

*D*r Voikin's tablets rendered me virtually comatose, and so it was quite late when I went down to the kitchen for breakfast.

Amélie sent me down to the library, where Anya was already at the table waiting for me.

'How's your arm, Nicholas? Did you sleep well in the end?'

She didn't wait for a reply but waved me to sit down opposite. Over coffee, she told me that Natalie had been sedated by Dr Voikin but not before he had discovered the motive for her attack on me.

Apparently, Natalya greatly valued what she referred to as our 'friendship' and so had been shocked to see Anya leaving my room, kissing me, while I stood semi-naked at the door. She had drawn all sorts of wrong conclusions from this and, coming as it did at the same time as one of her moments of malaise, had armed herself with a syringe from Dr Voikin's surgery and decided to avenge what she considered a betrayal on my part.

Anya assured me that it would not happen again and that it would not, in the long term, affect our pupil/master relationship, as it was most unlikely that Natalya, once recovered, would remember anything about it.

Today was Sunday, so I would have the day to myself.

Breakfast didn't appeal to me very much that morning and, as the spring sunshine was enticing me outside, I persuaded Agnès to make me a pot of coffee and went out to the small table under the lime trees bounded by the kitchen walls. This was a particularly bright suntrap, and I sat facing the brick garden path, listening to the hum of activity in the kitchen. The events of the previous night had shaken me up more than I cared to admit. I needed to calm down.

From my seat, I could look up at the windows of the rear of the House. Counting them along to the far corner of the third floor, I came to the ones where Natalie had told me the Grand Duchess had her suite. All the curtains were drawn but, as I squinted against the sunlight, I fancied that I saw a slight movement there, as if someone had been peeping at me and, caught out, quickly withdrawn.

The somewhat ungainly approach of Agnès, bearing a large coffee pot, distracted my attention, and, when I looked up at the windows again, all was still.

Agnès smiled shyly as she put down the coffee pot. Of all the 'staff', she seemed the most difficult to reach – mainly due to her lack of French, but also a natural reticence verging on secretiveness. Although young, she was also the least attractive of the women of the House, being big-boned and hard-featured, with frizzy blonde hair and a heavy red face that made her look as though she had been sitting too close to the fire. She was well-meaning, though, and seemed anxious to please.

Three cups of very bitter black coffee were enough, and I began to consider what I would do with my day. For the first time, I missed my old life in Paris – the sheer size of the place, the vibrant hum of life, the elegance. But to enjoy any of that you needed money, and I soon concluded that I was better off here at the House, at least for a while.

Gradually, I became aware that I wasn't feeling very well. My heart seemed to race and I began to feel restless and uneasy. Reasoning that it was perhaps too much strong coffee, or delayed shock from the previous night's traumatic events, I decided to go for a gentle walk and explore the garden and grounds.

At first I made good progress along the winding brick path, but, as I ventured deeper into the garden, I began to feel giddy and weak. To my left was a tall rose hedge and, behind this, offering a view of the lawns, was the small rose arbour I had found once before and, tottering slightly, I more or less collapsed on to the bench seat just inside.

I have always considered myself quite a healthy person, robust, and apart from the odd cold had never really been ill since moving to Paris. Soon to be twenty-three, I was at peak fitness, yet the uneasy fact remained that I had not felt well for some days – in fact, since coming to the House. Perhaps it was the food or, more likely, Serge's home-made vodka – although I was beginning to think there might be something in the tea that disagreed with me.

It was a beautiful day: the sun shone directly on to my bench, the garden air was fresh and bracing, and the birds flitted about just for the hell of it. Spring was definitely sprung, but I still felt odd – a sort of uneasiness, a feeling of detachment accompanied by drowsiness. I thought again that the shock of Natalie's frenzied attack was coming out in me. I determined to ignore my strange feelings and enjoy this beautiful day.

Eventually, however, the drowsiness must have overcome me, because I seemed to have drifted off.

Waking with a start, I sensed that I was no longer alone; facing me on the opposite bench sat a slim young lady in a crumpled white summer dress. Although I recognised her immediately as the girl I had seen before in the garden with her family in the distance, I could not prevent an involuntary start.

She seemed amused at this and fought to prevent her broad smile turning into a giggle.

I struggled to my feet, only half awake. '*Mademoiselle*…I'm sorry…'

'Please to sit down. It is I who should show regret…'

Her French was slow and rather quaint. I sat down and we looked at each other in silence. She impressed me with her naturalness: no make-up, long hair tied back in a loose bun and a simple white summer dress, long and emphasising her slim frame. She could not have been more than eighteen or nineteen. Her oval face held striking blue-grey eyes set off by high, Slavic cheekbones. She smiled nervously, showing small white teeth with a charming slight gap in the front. For all this rather rustic appearance and plain clothing, there was something rather regal about her – a presence and a sort of unassuming confidence.

The silence became uncomfortable, and finally she leaned closer to me and I was aware suddenly of a fragrance that I recognised immediately because my grandmother used to wear it and my mother sent me a sample when I first came to France and asked me to find some for her; it was Jasmin de Corse by Coty, a most popular perfume of the early 1900s but, sadly, unavailable after 1930.

'*Monsieur*…are you unwell?'

'Not really, it's just tiredness, I think.'

I tried to sound casual but I was really quite embarrassed, feeling oddly detached from my surroundings, as though I were observing the scene from somewhere else.

Suddenly she leaned closer and placed a cool dry hand on my forehead, seizing my wrist with her other hand, as if taking my pulse. It was all rather false, since she had no watch and missed my artery by at least an inch.

'Are you a nurse?' I asked, embarrassed and for want of anything else to say.

'No, not really – though I have nursed soldiers in 1916 during the Great War...' she added enthusiastically.

At the mention of the Great War, I began to have serious misgivings about my new companion's state of mind. Was everyone in this House eccentric? Were they all living in the same time-warp?

She had now finished her pretence of diagnosing my 'illness' and was studying me closely.

'You are not Russian, are you.' It was a statement and not a question.

'English,' I stated flatly.

'Oh, that's wonderful! I speak English too, and German, but not as well as Russian and French.'

'May I ask your name, in any of these languages?'

She smiled at me. 'You really don't know?' There was incredulity in her voice.

I shook my head and started an excuse: 'I'm new to this House –'

'This House?' She frowned for a moment, as though not understanding, and then announced grandly, 'Tatiana Nicolaevna Romanova, second daughter to the Tsar of all the Russias.'

Now I was certain that I was dealing with a fantasist.

'But you can call me Tanya, if we become friends, or even Tatianouchka; that's what the family call me. And you?'

'Nicholas,' I said warily.

'Do you prefer Nick or Nicky? It must be an honour for you to be named after my father...the Tsar, I mean.'

Charming and attractive as this girl was, I felt embarrassed at her evident confused mental state, and wondered whether she might be related to Natalya and share her inherited 'malaise'. Before I could formulate an answer, however, she stood up.

'Someone is coming. I must go. It was so nice to have met you, Nicholas. We must meet again.'

I rose and she gave me her hand. Feeling that I was now something of an old hand at this, I kissed it, clicked my heels and bowed in an old-fashioned way, expecting her to giggle. To my surprise, she remained serious, and took herself off quickly with what seemed like an air of practised 'imperial' aloofness, playing out her delusion to the end. Within four or five steps from the arbour, she had disappeared, leaving only the scent of Jasmin de Corse to mark her passing.

I sat down heavily, musing that, confined as it might be, life in this House was never dull. In just under one week, I'd been frightened half to death by the diva who was Madame Lili, stabbed by my pupil Princess Natalya, and subjected to the company of highly eccentric people who believed that they were living in an age fifty years earlier!

These thoughts were still in my mind when I heard Anya calling my name. She rounded the rose arbour and stood, blocking the sunlight, in front of me.

'There you are, Nicholas! I've looked everywhere for you.' She looked round, frowning. 'I heard your voice; who were you talking to?'

'Er…Tatiana.'

'Who's Tatiana?'

'You know – the Tsar's daughter.'

My attempt at levity misfired. Anya didn't laugh; in fact, she barely suppressed her annoyance. 'I'm not in the mood for jokes, Nicholas. Who was it?'

'Tatiana…at least, that's what she said! Calm down, Anya. We were only talking nonsense…'

'There *is* no "Tatiana" here. Who was she? Don't make me angry, Nico, I'm having a bad day.'

'Look, Anya, I'm having a bad day too. I really don't know who she was. She crept up here while I was dozing, told me I looked ill, and went through some pantomime about being a nurse in the "Great War". Then she crowned that, if you'll excuse the pun, by telling me that she was the second daughter of the Tsar – no, the "Tsar of all the Russias". I don't know any more about her – just another crackpot. You seem to have an endless supply of them around here.'

I regretted the remark as soon as I said it. Anya just glared at me. 'Where did she go?'

I pointed to the left but Anya was already moving quickly towards the House. Moments later, she reappeared with Serge and the two of them quickly began to search the grounds, with something approaching panic.

I went back to the kitchen and sat down to watch Amélie as she prepared lunch. After a while, Serge and Anya returned, Anya looking angry and flustered. She came over and plonked herself down near me. Serge did the same on the other side and I could hear her taking deep breaths as she sought to contain her anger.

At last she calmed down and even managed to smile at me, as you would humour a child you wanted to tell you a secret.

'Now, Nicholas. This is very important. Are you *sure* you don't know who she is?' she wheedled.

'No. Really. I just thought they must be neighbours or perhaps "inmates"…I mean, guests, here.'

The sarcasm went over her head. 'They?'

'Yes. The first time she was with her family; at least, I think that's who they were.'

'So you've seen her before?'

'Yes, but only in the distance…last week…but this is the first time we've spoken…'

'What did she speak to you? Was it Russian?'

'French.'

I didn't want to tell them I couldn't speak Russian. Anya and Serge exchanged glances. I felt I had to say something.

'Look, Anya, is there a problem here…er…with her? I mean, she was very charming but obviously quite mad – I mean, deluded.'

Anya forced an unconvincing smile. 'No, no. It's just that… the Grand Duchess doesn't like trespassers. You must promise us, Nico, that you will tell me straight away if you see her again.'

I nodded vigorously. They both got up and went out, leaving me alone with Amélie, who, I'd noticed, had been listening to our conversation. She eyed me anxiously and then, wiping her hands on her apron, went over to a small wooden box on a shelf near the pantry, took something out and then came back.

'Monsieur Nicholas, this is not of great value and it may not figure in your philosophy, but you would make me very happy if you were to wear it – all the time you are in this House.'

She held out a small ebony cross, the Russian Orthodox type, with two slanting cross-pieces; it was threaded on a leather bootlace.

'Er, thank you, Amélie. That's very kind.'

I felt embarrassed, but it was clear that she was waiting for me to put it on. She helped me fasten the leather thong. Then she sighed loudly, as if with relief. 'Monsieur Nicholas, please to take care of yourself.'

She stared directly at me for a moment and then went back to preparing lunch.

Anya seemed her old self over dinner in the kitchen that night, and the earlier tense atmosphere was soon replaced by the cheerful anticipation of good food followed by one of Sergei's 'soirées'.

About mid-evening, Agnès was called away by the bell from Madame Lili's room, and returned a few moments later to tell me that Madame Lili awaited me in the library.

In spite of her profession of friendship, I was still very wary of Madame Lili and her motives, and I approached the library with no little trepidation.

Beautiful as ever, Madame Lili was in a somewhat subdued mood. There was no effusive greeting and no exuberant exhortation to come to a séance, not even a dark warning about not believing; none of that. She forced a smile at me and then asked the same questions that I had already answered for Anya. I cast about desperately in my mind for something to say in answer, but all I could think of to tell Madame Lili was that I had identified the perfume she had worn. By now, I was beginning to wonder why my young and deluded new friend Tatiana (if that was really her name) had the ability to cause widespread dismay, even panic, in this staid and conservative community. No explanation was forthcoming, however, and again I was made to promise to report any future sightings as soon as possible. Then I was dismissed after the obligatory glass of tea.

Natalie's break-in the previous night had unnerved me more than I liked to admit, and I checked that all my doors were locked before blowing out the lamp. Tired as I was, sleep still came reluctantly to me, and was full of weird intrusions. 'Tatiana' flitted in and out of my dreams, sometimes as a nurse fussing around me and sometimes as a cold Imperial Majesty, disdainfully dismissing me. When I woke the next day, I felt tired and exhausted, and made a vow to keep off the Russian tea, especially at night.

# Chapter 6

# Osculation

*'And I find more bitter than death the woman whose heart is snares…'*

Ecclesiastes 7:26

In spite of all these weird goings-on, I was starting to feel that I was now part of the household; that somehow, grudgingly, the House was beginning to accept me and I would soon become one of the denizens of its dark corridors, splendid suites and warm, oil-lamp-lit rooms. Even the huge bathroom with its rusty pipes, massive iron bath and acres of cracked white tiles and porcelain basins and bowls was becoming acceptable, though it steamed up within minutes of running the clanking hot water system. The trick was to shave in the mirror before running the bath!

So I was feeling quite at home and, though the House still had its sinister places and harboured people who were, in the nicest interpretation, highly eccentric, it was the only fixed abode that I'd had for a long time, and the luxury of what really amounted to a small flat with 'staff' to look after me. Wearing smart clothes was also becoming second nature and, of course, there was plenty of time to study.

The only real downside was being unable to leave, even for a few hours, to go into central Paris, talk to my friends. But you can't have everything, can you?

My nicest surprise the next day was learning from Anya that Natalie was well enough to come to classes in the afternoon. I'd missed her much more than I liked to admit, and I was not angry with her, in the light of Anya's explanation for her attack on me. Actually, I thought it had given me a slight advantage. I mean, it was rather flattering that she felt we had a 'special' relationship, and also a little worrying that she seemed to be so obsessive about it. It seemed obvious to me that I should take great care over our future pupil/teacher relationship and certainly not give way to any feelings that I might have been starting to develop for her. Strictly business from now on, I decided, and wondered if she would express any regret for her actions. A royal apology would have been a first for me.

As two o'clock approached, I started to feel a little apprehensive. Images of Natalya being dragged away by Dr Voikin flooded back into my mind. Her pale face and bloodless lips, blue-grey eyes circled by dark lines – they would stay with me forever, etched into my mind by the shock I had received. Until that night, I hadn't realised how ill she was, hadn't understood how devastating her affliction could be.

A slight tapping on the schoolroom door brought me back to the present, and I hastened to let the Princess in, unsure what to expect.

I stood back in amazement at the image before me.

Natalya, dressed in a tight-fitting light grey two-piece suit, strode into the room amidst a gust of heavy perfume. Her eyes were bright and clear and she now had some colour in her face. Her short blonde hair hung like a golden curtain on one side of her face, almost concealing one eye, and, as she turned to face me, a dazzling white smile showed off her lovely teeth, clenched together slightly – a habit I had noticed also in Madame Lili. I supposed that gestures were easily picked up when people lived together for a long time and in such proximity.

If I had expected some sort of apology for the events of the night before last, I would have been disappointed. As it was, she took my breath away. Any connection between this elegant, strikingly beautiful young woman and the frightened, bedraggled child who had so recently attacked me would be impossible to conceive.

'Good afternoon, Monsieur Nicholas.' She smiled at me again with no hint of embarrassment.

'Good afternoon, Natalya,' I stuttered, still unsure how to address her.

She stepped closer and looked me straight in the eye. 'I have been so much anticipating the pleasure of your company for this lesson.'

Her English was impressive. She had obviously been practising her pronunciation.

'So have I…er…Natalie.'

It sounded stilted and formal. I didn't want to give the impression that I was in any way resentful of the other night.

She moved over to a chair and sat down, crossing her legs in a ladylike way, and I noticed, for the first time that she was wearing modern shoes.

She had chosen – deliberately, I thought – a seat in direct sunlight from the tall front windows and was as though in a spotlight, emphasising the beautiful symmetry of her classic features. She sat there, tall and slim, perched on the front edge of the chair, and looked up at me, still smiling, revealing the graceful curve of her neck.

She looked down at the floor for a long moment and when she looked up again her lips were parted and I could see the pink tip of her tongue poking slightly between her teeth. Then she tilted her head down, as if to study the book she was holding, but really to turn her eyes up at me, looking through half-closed eyelashes. It was a fascinating if somewhat naïve display, and it was not lost on me. She was flirting with me, in the most obvious way!

Perhaps I should have put a stop to it there and then, re-established the respect of the pupil/teacher relationship firmly and politely. But I did not. I was flattered and intrigued, and so I allowed her to continue, while pretending to ignore it. Hindsight is a wonderful thing.

'What's your book, Natalie?'

'Oh, it is an English novel of the Victorians. I have been, how you say…listing the vocabulary that I did not understand, to ask you to explain it to me.'

Her English accent was really very good and I knew I couldn't take credit for that, after such a short time. I wondered who my predecessor might have been.

There followed a brief discussion about the various pronunciations of words ending in '-ough' and Natalie laughed at the complexity of it and my obvious inability to explain it or provide a grammatical rule for her to follow.

'You just have to learn as you go along,' I told her, lamely.

'Like life, I think,' she said archly, standing up suddenly and producing a piece of paper with vocabulary she must have noted from her Victorian novel. 'Monsieur Nicholas, please to explain. What means "osculate"?'

'Oscillate?'

'No. Osculate.'

To my embarrassment I couldn't place the word at all, and admitted, sheepishly, that I did not know. To hide my embarrassment, I made a show of taking down the huge Oxford dictionary and looking up the word.

'"Osculate…poetic, from the Latin meaning 'to kiss'."'

I read it out loud and, when I stopped, I realised that Natalie was standing close behind me. She put her hands on my shoulders and gently pulled me round to face her. Her closeness intimidated me but I made no move to pull away.

'So now, Nicholas, will you osculate with me?'

I'd fallen into a trap.

She leaned her face close to mine, pursed her lips and closed her eyes. My brain went into neutral; I couldn't move and I couldn't speak, unable even to formulate a simple thought. We stood like that for what seemed an age and nothing happened. Suddenly, she opened her eyes wide and, blushing with embarrassment, stepped back.

'Oh, Monsieur Nicholas, forgive me. I have made a large mistake…!'

A tear ran from the corner of her eye. And that did it. I leaned forward, put my arm around her fragile waist and kissed her; a long, heartfelt kiss that was my second step on the road to disaster.

After that initial kiss, Natalie had complete control of the situation. Her naïveté seemed to vanish and she took my hand and pulled me through into the small room that served both as my sitting room and study; then she headed straight to my bedroom.

Every step we took broke down my resolve and yet, even as she pulled me down beside her on the bed, my conscience was screaming 'No!'

But I had ceased to listen to my brain; my body was calling to me now, and its needs and desires overrode all reason.

The fragrance of her youthful body intoxicated me and the touch of her gentle yet urgent hands sent little shocks of pleasure through my skin. She was no longer the shy, bashful, aloof Natalya I had seen only moments before, and I wondered at the sudden change from coy, naïve teenager to determined young woman. It was almost as if she knew what to do and what to expect of me, yet how could she have had any experience of romance in this sterile House?

It is impossible for me to describe adequately the pleasure I felt – we felt – in each other. Everything seemed to proceed so naturally, so easily, as though we had rehearsed it in our heads a thousand times; as though, even when we were behaving formally in the classroom, this more intimate scene was running in our minds. It sounds so stupid now, but it was almost like a *déjà vu* experience for both of us.

Without any embarrassment, awkwardness or even word spoken, we climaxed together, and it was – at least for me – the release of my pent-up desire and longing for this young woman. I had the sense to enjoy it to the full before the guilt and remorse that I knew would inevitably follow.

I hoped that I wasn't rough with her. She seemed so slim and delicate that I was afraid of holding her too tightly and hurting her. In fact, I scarcely behaved as a gentleman should, such was my longing for her. I tried to make up for it by being attentive and considerate afterwards. To my intense relief, Natalie did not appear to have been made uncomfortable in any way. I had never made love to a virgin before and had expected it to be different somehow. But Natalie seemed to have enjoyed it as much as I did and, as we both lay exhausted across my bed, she took my hand and kissed it, making little sighing noises which I understood to be pleasure.

Neither of us spoke for a long time. We both knew that everything had changed now. The line had been crossed. The guilt was creeping over me, as I had known it would, and only then did I start to deal with realities. I was her tutor: she should have been able to rely on me to make sensible decisions, do sensible things to protect her, look after her. Instead, I had taken her virginity. What if she got pregnant?

I sat up abruptly, startling Natalie, who seemed on the verge of sleep.

'Nicholas? What's wrong?' She sat up too, eyes full of questions. What could I tell her? That her lover was a stupid, inconsiderate idiot? That he was so selfish that he had given no thought to the consequences of his actions? It was too late now to think of all that. There was no form of contraception available to us in that House, and I wasn't about to ask Natalie about her menstrual cycle and suchlike, even if I had understood it myself.

Mercifully, this train of thought was broken by Natalie herself when she looked at her watch and realised that she must go.

We dressed in silence, picking up the articles of clothing we had discarded between the schoolroom and the bed. The hurried kiss goodbye seemed awkward and embarrassed and then she was gone, and, with her, the sunlight.

After Natalya left, I sat down on the sofa in my small study next to the fire and thought about the future. To have kissed Natalie was one thing; to have made love to her was, frankly, a shock, and changed things irrevocably. If I could have been honest with myself, I should have admitted that I was falling in love with this girl. All the signs were there; I just chose to ignore them because I didn't know how to deal with the problem. It was typical of my conduct in general, drifting about in Paris, no fixed address, few close friends and no special girl.

I got up and walked about the room. This was definitely a no-win situation. To pursue an 'affair' with my pupil was strictly not on, and once it was revealed I would certainly be dismissed. If that happened, I would not be able to see Natalie again. On the other hand, how could I not respond to her when, in spite of every obstacle, I had fallen in love with her?

Finally I resolved to do what I always did – let it go, stop thinking about it. Something would happen, and it would all come right in the end. It was a frame of mind I'd inherited from my father, a fatalism that seemed to fit in well with my study of existentialism. In any case, I could see no alternative.

Having dismissed the business of the mind, I then considered the needs of the body. I was elated but I was also hungry; the two things always went together with me and, although it was only 4.30pm, I showered and went down to the kitchen to seek some company.

No one seemed surprised to see me so early, and it appeared almost as if they were expecting me. When I enquired about dinner, they looked at one another and smiled.

I hate conspiracies. 'Did I say something amusing, Serge?' I asked, trying to keep the note of annoyance out of my voice.

'Not at all, Nicolai Feodorovitch. You obviously have not been told—'

'Told what?' I cut in, a bit abruptly.

'You and Anya are eating with the Grand Duchess tonight.' Seeing my consternation, he continued quickly, 'I hope you have your dinner suit ready.'

A murmur of amusement swept the kitchen.

'I don't have an evening dress suit…' I said in dismay.

'Yes, you do, Nico. I have it here.'

It was Anya, framed in the doorway, a package in her arms.

'You remember, Nicholas, when I interviewed you, I said suits would be supplied? Well, here is your evening wear. You'd better try it on. Dinner is at 8pm in the great dining room. I'll collect you from your rooms at 7.30.'

She pushed the parcel into my arms and was gone. The others looked on in amusement and I beat a hasty retreat to my rooms to get out of their way.

The suit fitted perfectly, as the others had done: black, double-breasted, with old-fashioned wide lapels faced with shiny black silk. I'd never actually owned a dinner suit. The ones I'd worn in the past were always hired from Moss Bros – for Ladies' Nights at my father's lodge in London – and returned the next day.

I managed everything, including the cummerbund, but was beaten by the bow tie and old-style butterfly collar on the dress shirt, being used to the modern clip-on bows. When she came to fetch me Anya tied it for me and then we both sat, self-consciously, in the library to await the summons to dinner.

# CHAPTER 7

# The Séance

*'Fear came upon me, and trembling, which made all my bones to shake. Then a Spirit passed before my face; the hair of my flesh stood up. It stood still, but I could not discern the form thereof…'*

JOB 4:14–16

It was with considerable misgiving that I walked past the right-hand staircase towards the great dining room. Anya held my arm and, though her presence was reassuring, I felt uneasy and uncomfortable. Madame Lili would be there, and meeting her had so far been an ambivalent experience. She was, beyond doubt, a most alluring and bewitching woman, yet at the same time she was capable of causing me 'fear and trembling', as it says in the Bible. As for the Grand Duchess, she was treated with such respect – even reverence – by those around her that she was bound to intimidate me. Added to all this was the discomfort I felt from wearing such formal clothes. No doubt every part of my behaviour and conversation would be scrutinised by the other guests.

I need not have worried. We were told on entering the room that unfortunately the Grand Duchess was slightly indisposed and would not be joining us. I was able to relax slightly.

The dining room was huge and impressive, comprising most of the right wing of the ground floor. The whole front wall was taken up by floor-to-ceiling windows covered, although it was still daylight outside, with heavy and elaborate crimson curtains. Oil lamps hung overhead and from brackets on the walls, casting a bright yet soft glow and giving off a faint smell of lamp oil. As expected, in spite of the warm spring evening a coal fire burned in the grate of the huge marble fireplace. The brightness of the room was increased by a huge silver candelabrum in the centre of the white linen tablecloth, its light glinting off the silver settings and cut-glass vases of fresh flowers.

Anya introduced me to two elderly men, who clicked their heels and bowed in an old-fashioned, Eastern European way. The first, who vaguely resembled an old photograph I had once seen of Dr Crippen, was a man in his sixties with a white moustache and grey hair – it was Dr Voikin, whom I had met very briefly when he and Serge had dragged Natalie off me on the night of the attack. As well as being Natalie's personal doctor, he also looked after the Grand Duchess and had a surgery in the right wing of the House, where he sometimes slept when twenty-four-hour care was required.

The second man was much taller, and so thin that he looked as though he might need the good doctor's services himself. His thinning, oily hair was dyed black, his cheeks hollow, and long face drawn, giving an overall impression of furtive deceit. He was introduced as Maître Chermakov, and the fact that he was the family lawyer did not surprise me at all.

Neither man qualified as congenial company. The women were much more interesting.

Madame Lili was, as usual, all in black, her heavy silk dress falling to almost cover her buttoned-up boots; a sort of lifted-up veil covered her hair, which was piled up on top of her head, revealing her pale, aristocratic face and the intense darkness of her eyes. As I stepped forward to greet her and kiss her proffered hand, she parted her lips slightly and narrowed her eyes in a penetrating glance. It would not have surprised me if those big white teeth had included fangs.

Natalya, however, looked much more welcoming, resplendent in a long, cream silk dress with matching gloves and shoes. She wore her hairpiece that night, piled up on her head and then cascading down her back, soft and honey-coloured in the glow of the oil lamps. A narrow black velvet band circled her graceful neck, and a small gold locket hung down from it to her throat.

She treated me to a long, warm smile and fixed me with her blue-grey eyes as if to convey a sort of complicity that marked us out as different from the others. She took my arm in a possessive way and, with Anya on the other side, drew me to my place at the far end of the table, directly facing Madame Lili who, in the absence of the Grand Duchess, assumed her place at the head of the group – a gesture of superiority which seemed to be acceptable to all the others present.

I was disappointed to find that both Natalya and Anya were separated from me by the presence of the two men, and surprised to learn that there would be no other guests, except a certain Father Feodor, who was expected later.

To my relief, dinner was served and eaten in an almost informal way and everyone, including my somewhat taciturn male companions, engaged in an attempt at small talk. Of the two, Dr Voikin proved to be the most affable, though he had little competition from Maître Chermakov, who seemed to be struggling to conceal his obvious dislike of dinner engagements. No mention was made of any of the recent events in the House, other than the doctor enquiring, out of politeness, whether my 'malaise' had passed. The lawyer confined himself to a few questions about my family and background, posed with little subtlety, and my answers were not received with great good grace.

The food was excellent, however, and had the men not been there the evening could have been quite pleasant.

The meal finished and the men, myself included, withdrew to the far end of the room and both Voikin and Chermakov lit cigarettes. In spite of disliking smoke, I felt obliged to stand with them, and cast around for something to say during the awkward silence that ensued. Not daring to discuss Natalya's illness, I settled finally on asking after the health of the somewhat mysterious and elusive Grand Duchess.

Voikin eyed me suspiciously and then reluctantly offered, 'For her age, she is well. She is currently indisposed. Not serious, I think, but something that may be expected at her time of life. Nothing *you* should concern yourself about,' he added, fixing me with another hard look and emphasising the word 'you'. 'And yourself, *monsieur*?' he deftly changed the subject, continuing, 'I recall treating you last week…some symptoms of giddiness, wasn't it?' He didn't wait for a reply but dismissed his own enquiry by adding, 'I assume you are better now?'

I was still considering whether I should tell him that I was actually feeling much worse, and should perhaps detail the strange feelings of detachment that were becoming more frequent, when Chermakov gestured towards Natalya and Anya. 'They seem to wish you to join them.'

His relief at this showed on his face. Both women were looking towards us, smiling, and giving me an excuse to leave the two lugubrious old fossils who obviously preferred each other's company.

Both women seemed to be enjoying themselves: as I drew near them, I could hear their animated chatting in French. In fact, no one in the House ever seemed to speak Russian. Anya had once told me that the Grand Duchess had forbidden it, saying that French was the language of the Russian Court and Russian was only to be used to address the servants. Even the 'servants' spoke French all the time, albeit with varying degrees of fluency. As I listened, I was again intrigued by the distinctly Germanic accents of Natalie and Madame Lili. Only Anya spoke French without a German accent. 'How chic you look, Nicholas!' Natalie whispered in my ear, and squeezed my hand. 'It gives me great sorrow to have to leave you, but the Grand Duchess has asked me to read to her. It helps her with the sleeping,' she said quaintly. She turned her back to the others, winked at me and, after making excuses to the other guests and giving a quick glance back over her shoulder to me, left the room.

My disappointment must have shown in my face, because Anya drew me aside and whispered that the real reason for Natalie's absence was her dislike of all things spiritual or occult. By this time, Agnès and Serge had cleared the tables of everything except the candelabrum, and it was then that I learned we were going to have a séance and Anya's talk about the occult made sense.

In spite of my total scepticism, I felt excited at the prospect of watching Madame Lili perform; an excitement tinged with uneasiness as I recalled the troubling effect she had previously wrought on me.

We took our places as directed by Anya, but Natalie's seat to my immediate left was now empty. No one spoke. Madame Lili sat at the head of the table, pale and serious and, I was surprised to see, seemed tense and perhaps a little nervous. She stared down at the white tablecloth and appeared to be composing herself, sitting perfectly still and breathing deeply.

As Agnès quietly left the room, Serge, who had earlier disappeared, re-entered, resplendent in high boots and cavalry breeches and wearing a white *rubashka*, a Russian shirt, embroidered with classic blue and gold at the neck and cuffs.

He was, though, bare-headed, his Cossack hat not to be worn indoors.

Extinguishing the oil lamps one by one, he eventually arrived at the table and there snuffed out all but the central candle of the candelabrum. Gradually my eyes became accustomed to the dim light and I noticed that Serge was now standing impassively behind Madame Lili like a sort of élite bodyguard. It was Dr Voikin, an unlikely convert to spiritualism it seemed to me, who stood up and recited a prayer for divine guidance for what he referred to as 'Our undertaking, this night'.

Those around the table to the left and right of me remained only just discernible in the dim light emanating from the lone candle in the centre of the table, but everything beyond our circle was now in complete darkness.

At some point, Father Feodor must have entered the room – he had not been there at dinner – and was just visible seated to Madame Lili's right. He stood up, appearing sinister in what could be seen of his dark robes and hat, and intoned what I took to be a prayer in Russian, then produced what looked like a silver tube with holes in it and sprinkled water around the table.

Next, it was the turn of Madame Lili. She took up a small sack that contained white powder, presumably salt, and drew a circle around the single candle. Closing her eyes, she murmured slowly in French, 'Spirits of the Dead, pass among us. Be guided by this light of our World and visit upon us.'

She then sat down, leaned back in her chair and closed her eyes.

Sceptic and atheist that I was, I could at least applaud the setting and drama of the piece. The atmosphere was somehow disturbing, the air suddenly cooler. I found myself wishing that Natalie were sitting beside me.

Someone familiar with the proceedings, probably Voikin, must have given the signal to link hands. To my right, though I could barely make him out in the darkness, Chermakov grasped my hand in a moist, bony grip. To my left, I could not reach across the empty seat to find Anya and wondered, stupidly, if by not completing the circle I might impede the success of the séance.

No one remarked on this and I guessed they could not see that the circle was broken. I felt too intimidated to speak.

It was strange how the circle of light thrown by the candle seemed to become smaller and dimmer. Anya to my far left and even Chermakov next to me on the right were barely discernible, and Voikin and Serge were in complete darkness. Only Madame Lili was clearly visible, and I wondered how she seemed to attract all the light. She appeared to be sleeping, with her eyes closed, and chin on her chest, without the slightest movement.

After what seemed to be a long time, I fancied that I could hear her breathing heavily and gradually faster. Inwardly, I admired the theatrical effects except…except…I was beginning to feel more and more uneasy in spite of my dismissal of the whole business as a sham. An involuntary shiver ran down my back and I felt oddly cold and uncomfortable. Slowly at first, the solitary candle started to flicker, and then to gutter and dim as though about to go out.

Suddenly, Madame Lili opened her eyes wide and, staring straight down the table, gasped out, 'Something is coming! It is here, amongst us!'

The look of horror on her face intimidated me by its genuineness and I felt my whole body tense. Absolute silence reigned in the huge room, now reduced to just this table and feeble candle glow.

Gradually, I became aware of vague movement to my left. First, a slight draught disturbed the air, then there was a faint rustling sound and slight creaking, as if someone had just sat down in the chair beside me. A fragrance filled the air, a perfume that seemed somehow familiar.

My whole body flinched as something grasped my left hand and I started, involuntarily, before my brain realised that Natalie must have slipped back into the room and, somehow, in the dark, found her seat beside me. Now her cool hand grasped mine and I felt a gentle squeeze of the fingers by way of a silent greeting.

Madame Lili, meanwhile, seemed horrified at whatever she believed was taking place. She continued to stare down the table and seemed to be focused on the seat beside me. Slowly, she lifted her hand and pointed to my left. Her long, gloved fingers trembled and a look of both surprise and real horror froze her face.

Even as I watched, fascinated, I was becoming aware that something was not as it seemed. The hand in mine was not gloved and there were rings on the fingers. The perfume... was Jasmin de Corse...this was *not* Natalya! My brain screamed it at me and I made to snatch my hand away, but I seemed paralysed at this realisation and unable even to utter the cry rising in my throat. Time seemed to stop and then, suddenly, the hand let go. The guttering candle suddenly flared up and for a few seconds lighted the table before dying and plunging us into total darkness. And, in that one short flicker of light, I understood everything. There, in the chair beside me, though her face was averted, I had just time to discern the long white dress and auburn hair of Tatiana, the girl I had met in the garden and who had told me in her charming French that she was the second daughter of the Tsar of all the Russias – Tatiana Nicolaevna Romanova.

Nor was I the only one to recognise her; Serge, still invisible in the darkness behind Madame Lili, gasped out loud, '*Velikaya Knyazhna!*' – Your Highness!

Absolute silence followed and then all hell broke loose. I felt, rather than saw, Chermakov jump to his feet. Voikin must have done the same. A chair scraped and the table juddered violently. I heard Anya screaming.

'Oh, my God, she was holding my hand!'

There was the sound of movement, footsteps muffled by the carpet, and then the room lit up as I had never seen it. Serge, overriding the instructions from the Grand Duchess never to use the electric lights, had somehow got to the door and found the switch next to it.

We all blinked in the sudden dazzling light, and when I was able to focus I saw that the chair next to me was overturned and there was no sign of Tatiana in the room.

Madame Lili remained seated, a look of total bewilderment on her beautiful face. The two men stood a few feet back from the table, seemingly paralysed, and Anya had begun to hyperventilate, teetering on the verge of hysteria. Father Feodor was on his knees, muttering and crossing himself.

Only Serge, standing by the light switch at the door, seemed in control of himself. He looked at me and shouted above Anya's shrieks, 'Nicolai Feodorovitch, was that the person you saw in the grounds?'

I nodded.

'Come with me, we must search the House.'

It was an order, from a Cossack. I went with him, more shocked at the general panic than surprised at seeing Tatiana.

As we ran up the stairs, I remembered the consternation that had greeted my earlier description of meeting her in the rose arbour and the near panic that had ensued on that occasion. There was, however, no time to dwell on those thoughts as I followed Serge in his frantic search from room to room.

I don't know how long it took to search the whole House but eventually we returned, wearily, to the dining room. As soon as we entered, Madame Lili looked up and interrogated Serge with her eyes. Slowly, he shook his head and Madame

Lili turned her eyes on me. Instead of her usual penetrating gaze, I thought I could discern an almost pleading appeal for an explanation, and I realised in that moment that, whatever had just taken place in front of us, it was not Madame Lili's doing. For once, she seemed to have lost control of events. She could not understand what had just happened, and it frightened her.

She got up and moved slowly towards me. The usual intimidating presence, the steely self-confidence, was gone. Instead I saw a beautiful but suddenly vulnerable and bewildered woman.

'Help me, Nicholas,' she whispered.

'Of course, Madame Lili,' I replied, seizing my chance and taking the proffered gloved hand. She was trembling slightly and, in spite of the fact that she had, some might say deliberately, frightened me in the past, my heart went out to her now.

We were interrupted by Dr Voikin, who, assisted by Chermakov, was trying to half-walk, half-carry a sobbing Anya from the room. Madame Lili went to help them and they all stumbled out into the passage together, leaving just the stolid Serge and myself in the room. He moved to the door and then looked back at me.

'Come on, come to the kitchen.'

He nodded in the direction of the back of the House and made the universal gesture of drinking from a glass. I followed, lamely, with a last glance back into the empty room with its upturned chairs, deserted table and burned-out candle.

Serge grunted as he looked across at me.

'You know more about this than you're saying, Nicolai Feodorovitch.'

We were both sprawled in chairs next to the fireplace, a glass of his 'special' vodka in hand. This was not the first glass, and the fierce liquid, together with the heat from the fire and the physical exertion of searching the whole House, had had their effect on us. Serge's new *rubashka* was now undone, as was his belt. I had long since discarded my jacket and bow tie and unbuttoned the uncomfortable fly collar. Both of us had propped our feet up on the fender.

'Well?' he prompted.

'Look, Serge, I know only what I've already told you. I met this girl when I was sitting in the arbour, just yesterday. I was asleep so I don't know where she came from – she was just *there* beside me when I woke up… I'd not been feeling well, if you remember. She told me she'd been a nurse in the Great War and pretended to take my pulse…'

'What language did she speak?'

'French and a bit of English, as I remember.'

'No Russian?'

'Not that I recall, though her French had a distinct Russian accent…'

I didn't want to admit that I couldn't speak Russian. He looked at me sternly and arched his eyebrows into a frown. 'What else did she say?'

'Only that she was called Tatiana and that her father was the Tsar.'

Serge eyed me with suspicion before leaning forward and asking, 'You are sure about that, my son?'

It was the first time he had called me 'son'.

'Yes, I'm sure. I'll tell you something, though, Serge. She's definitely not a ghost or a spirit. When she held my hand, she was warm flesh and blood.'

He grunted, picked up the bottle and poured us each another shot, stared into the fire and then turned slowly to face me. His voice was hoarse. 'That's as maybe, but she didn't come past me to get to the door, so where did she go?'

'You saw her, Serge. We all saw her. She *was* there. Anyway, what's all the fuss about? It made for an interesting evening, didn't it?'

'Oh, you laugh now, Nicolai Feodorovitch, but I saw your face when I put the lights on and you were scared then.'

I didn't know how to reply to that, and anyway I was fed up with constantly being interrogated by everyone. The vodka having done its work, I decided to call it a night. Serge, I knew, would sit up all night nursing that bottle, but I was all in. Making my excuses, I shuffled off to bed.

I wasn't so tired though that I didn't turn the whole thing over in my mind once I'd locked the doors, got into bed and blown out the candle.

My mind immediately returned to the séance. It had not been at all what I'd expected. No raps, no levitating chairs or tables, no spirit guide for Madame Lili to consult, and no nebulous spirit forms hovering above us and playing trumpets. Where was the protective circle with its pentagrams and magic symbols into which we all cowered when the Rider of the Pale Horse of the Apocalypse (whose name was Death) assailed us?

Disappointment was my first reaction, but Serge's words echoed in my mind: 'She didn't come past me to get to the door, so where did she go?'

Finally, I slipped into an uneasy, troubled sleep.

# CHAPTER 8

# Hallucinosis

*'"Won't you come into my parlour?" said the spider to the fly…'*

It must have been the early hours of the morning when I awoke, or at least became vaguely aware of my surroundings. It was pitch dark but warm and comfortable in bed, and a relaxed drowsiness overcame me.

A beautiful perfume pervaded the room and I sensed rather than felt the person beside me. Natalie! She must have come to me, as if in answer to my dreams, as if in answer to the disappointment of her absence most of the evening.

Still only half awake, I reached out to her and felt her snuggle into my arms with a small sigh of pleasure. Tired, and a bit drunk, I would have slipped back into sleep had she not gradually aroused me with gentle movements of her body. Soon, in spite of my befuddled state, I was reaching over to kiss her…a strange, tight-lipped, even bashful kiss from her that surprised me. Sitting up, I gently rolled her on to her back and began the moves that precede lovemaking – slow and tender. Any inhibitions I might once have felt had evaporated with the passion of our previous lovemaking, and I was soon awake enough to take the lead and begin to make love to her.

She seemed strangely unresponsive, as if she wanted to but had forgotten how, and seemed awkward and gauche, eager yet hesitant. It was not until we climaxed and were lying exhausted together that these separate clues began to assemble in my befuddled brain.

I sat up with a suddenness that jolted the bed, peered down at her in the thick darkness and the awful truth hit me: this was not Natalie! The scent of jasmine, the strange kiss, the awkward lovemaking...but, even as I thought these things, the truth dawned on me:

'Tatiana?'

I felt rather than saw her nod her head.

'Oh, Nicholas! Do you really love me? You know you are the first...the only...' she whispered in her quaint accented French.

I leapt out of bed. I don't know what I thought I was going to do. My confusion was absolute. I groped for the bedside table...the candle...the matches, but even as I struck the flame I knew the bed was empty.

My first impulse was to run to the door and pursue her down the hall. Only my naked state and acute embarrassment prevented me, and I sank down on the bed, overcome by the enormity of what I had just done-- the betrayal of Natalya and the compromising of Tatiana.

Even while she was still being sought by everyone in the House, I was 'sleeping with the enemy'.

Suddenly cold, I slipped into bed and lay back on the pillow as the events of the night churned in my mind.

In the end, I took the coward's way out. I determined to keep quiet about everything and hope that it would all go away. After all, no one knew about it – except, of course, Tatiana – and she had no contact with anyone else in the House so no one could know unless I told them. The alternative was to confess to Natalie that it had all been a mistake, that I had been tricked into it. That seemed like a recipe for disaster, though, and, even if Natalie did understand and forgive me, what would Madame Lili make of the whole thing? No. Best be silent.

Sleep would not return and I was glad to go down to breakfast. Even then, I was half expecting trouble. What if Tatiana had been seen leaving my room? Where did she go without any clothes, and where was she now? Had I upset her deeply? I would not have done that for the world. But there was no way to find her and tell her.

Serge grunted a half-hearted return greeting. In spite of all the vodka, he looked bright and alert.

'Stuff and nonsense!' he shouted, fixing me with a frown. 'Séances…superstitious rubbish, all of it. Spirits from the dead, my arse…'

'Serge!' It was Anya, standing by the door. 'Please moderate your language!'

Serge looked sheepish and mumbled his excuses but he wasn't done. 'You'll be telling me next that she was a ghost.'

He had obviously been ruminating about the night before. I couldn't resist a taunt.

'It was you standing by the door, Serge. What did you say to me when she disappeared? "She didn't come past me, so where did she go?"'

He reacted badly, jumping up and growling, 'I'm going outside…things to do. Stuff and nonsense.'

He slammed the door. Anya flashed me a quick, embarrassed smile. She seemed completely recovered from the previous evening's shock.

'So what do you make of all this, Nicholas?'

I prevaricated. 'It was my first séance, Anya. I didn't know what to expect...'

'But you've seen the girl before, haven't you, in the garden, wasn't it? On Sunday. So you sort of know her. Do you think you could be psychic?'

She came over and sat across the table from me, leaned forward and stared me straight in the eyes. 'I think you know more about this mystery woman than you are telling us, Nicolai Feodorovitch.'

I didn't reply, sick and tired of the same old questions from everyone. She continued, 'Madame Lili thinks so too. She wants to see you this evening, Nicholas, in her rooms.'

Having delivered this summons with suitable sinister foreboding, Anya got up to leave. At the door, she turned and said archly, 'Good luck, Nico.'

Out of the corner of my eye, I saw Amélie the cook, get up from her usual seat beside the fire.

'Monsieur Nicholas, are you wearing the cross I gave you?'

'Uh, no, Amélie. I usually do, but I took it off when I showered this morning,' I lied.

She eyed me anxiously and came very close.

'Be sure to wear it tonight!' she whispered fiercely.

For the first time since arriving at the House, I was relieved to receive word that Natalie could not attend classes that day. Apparently, the Grand Duchess was still indisposed and wanted her company.

I didn't know how I could have faced her that day. Deeply ashamed at cheating on her, I sought refuge by telling myself that there was no way I could have known that the girl in my bed was Tatiana. But in my heart I knew that, even if I had realised earlier than I did, I would still have continued the lovemaking. There was no valid excuse, only a combination of events which had confused me until things had gone too far to stop. I was so selfish! It was not my proudest moment. My stay in this House was revealing some very nasty home truths.

More worrying was how to deceive Madame Lili if she asked me this evening about my relationship with the girl at the séance. I felt like a man condemned to be exposed as a liar and a cheat.

The apprehension didn't leave me all day, and I found myself taking deep breaths as I knocked on Madame Lili's door. Stupid really: what could she do to me that was any worse than asking me to leave the House? And why should she do that just because I happened to be the only person there who knew anything about Tatiana?

Her heavy perfume hit me as soon as she opened the door and stood back, smiling to let me enter. Mastering my unease, I couldn't help but admire the setting. This was Madame Lili as I had never seen her before. Instead of the long black dress, veil and big hat, she was breathtaking in a cream-coloured creation that was something between a sari and a bathrobe, trailing on the floor but with a slit on one side all the way up to her waist, showing her long, slim legs as she walked back towards the centre of the room. Her long black hair, usually piled high on her head in a sort of bun, hung in heavy curls about her shoulders and down her back and she moved sensuously to a chaise longue in the middle of the room, which was warm from the fire and softly lit with oil lamps. Adding to this heavy atmosphere were huge vases of lilies and freesias dotted about the room.

She sat on the chaise and patted a small armchair directly opposite and gestured to me to sit down. 'Ah, Nicolai Feodorovitch, how good of you to come. I have looked forward to this meeting all day.' She smiled up at me as I sat down. 'Bring your chair closer,' she urged. 'Let me look at you. No bad dreams, I hope, because of our little séance?'

I mumbled something about having enjoyed the evening, which she ignored. Leaning closer, she took both my wrists in her gloved hands and looked me full in the face. Again, I was struck by the dark, almost violet colour of her irises and her unblinking stare.

'Now, listen to me, Nicholas, listen to my voice…'

Another attempt to hypnotise me, as before, but I was ready for it this time and looked away, risking her anger. To my surprise she laughed and tutted.

'I didn't mean to intimidate you, Nico. Why are you so shy with me? We are friends, are we not?'

I forced myself to look at her again and nodded.

'I'm pleased about that. I thought, just for a moment, that you were upset with me. You know, Nico, I wouldn't want that to happen, because I've always considered that we have a "special" relationship.'

She leaned even closer, her face almost touching mine, and again gave me that long, slow smile, her white teeth parted, lips open and the pink tip of her tongue just visible between them.

'I wanted to ask you…' her voice dropped to a husky whisper '…to tell me about the girl…'

She was so close now that our noses almost touched, and all the time she held my wrists tightly – painfully tightly. In spite of my earlier resolve not to be intimidated by her, I felt my resistance ebbing away. My mind was becoming confused and I felt light-headed, almost dizzy.

'I…I really don't know that much about her. I…'

I didn't want to say that I was sick and tired of the same interrogation by all and sundry.

Suddenly, she turned her face to one side and put her mouth on mine, a long, hard kiss that killed my words and shocked me to the core. This lady, who so intimidated me and who seemed always so aloof and reserved, was kissing me with an intensity that I had never before experienced. Unwilling and unable to move, scarcely able to breathe, I sat rigid and unresponsive. She broke away.

'Madame Lili –'

Again, she cut my words off with her mouth. I felt her hands leave my wrists at last, only to feel them around my neck, pulling my head against hers so that there was no escape.

But I no longer wanted to escape. The dam inside me broke, and all my pent-up feelings of desire for her overwhelmed me. I returned her kiss with a ferociousness that amazed me. For a moment, I felt her tense and hesitate, and then she too seemed to give way and become soft and compliant in my arms.

Quite what happened then, I will probably never know. I've no idea how, but we found ourselves on the floor, Madame Lili's long legs wrapped around me, her hands ripping my shirt open.

When it happened, there was nothing gentle and graceful about it; nor was it 'romantic' or caring and considerate. It was sheer animal passion on both sides. I just remember climaxing in long, shuddering gasps, followed by concentric circles of a pleasure greater than any before; and hearing Madame Lili call my name again and again, her eyes closed and beads of perspiration on her lovely face.

Eventually we ceased to move together, yet the waves of pleasure continued to engulf me. Slowly, very slowly, they ebbed away, and I somehow managed to use my arms to lift my weight off her soft, limp body. Rolling on to my back, I just lay there, gasping for breath, while Madame Lili caressed my face with her gloved hand.

Instead of gradually clearing, my mind became more confused and for what seemed like an age I just stared at the blurred image of the room, trying to make sense of the situation.

I don't remember us getting up from the carpet or anything we did or said until I became aware that I was sprawled in the armchair once again and Madame Lili was no longer there. Still I made no attempt to get up, although I remember struggling to do up my clothes.

Only vaguely do I remember seeing her emerge from a small dressing room near the entrance to her room. She was fully dressed and her hair was now piled up on her head, revealing her slender white shoulders. She looked calm and collected and every inch the aristocrat. The merest smile emphasised the delicacy of her face and high cheekbones.

'I brought you something, Nicholas,' she said in a low husky voice, handing me a tall frosted champagne flute. 'Drink it now, all of it. It will refresh you.'

It was almost an order but I didn't need much persuasion. Cold and beautifully dry, the champagne was just what I needed. Or so I thought. It went down with indecent speed, only to be replaced by another from a small tray she was holding.

She sat down and patted my knee and I felt that it was a sort of thank you for the pleasure of our lovemaking, though she did not mention that at all. In fact, she behaved almost as if it hadn't happened, and we were back to business as usual. Except that I was not feeling 'as usual': my light-headedness was increasing and I began to have that old feeling of being detached from my surroundings. Grasping the arms of the chair, I took deep breaths to try to ward off the giddiness that was creeping over me. It was as if my mind had slipped into neutral and I could not focus my thoughts on anything and was waiting for Madame Lili to tell me what to do next.

I didn't have to wait long.

'Now, Nicholas, tell me all about "Tatiana" – everything this time. Do not leave anything out. Do you understand me?'

Her peremptory tone startled me. I supposed I'd had the carrot and now it was time for the big stick. At the same time, I felt oddly anxious to please her. I struggled to know where to start and she prompted me impatiently.

'Come along, Nicholas – you don't want to upset me, do you?'

I opened my mouth and then closed it again, deciding not to risk her anger, but still not knowing quite what to say.

Madame Lili leaned closer and, to my utter astonishment, delivered a stinging slap across my face, making me blink. 'I'm waiting, Nicolai Feodorovitch,' she hissed, her dark eyes flashing and her face suddenly thrust so close to mine that I jerked back involuntarily.

'I don't know what more I can tell you, Madame Lili… I saw her in the garden a couple of times, as I said. I don't know where she lives or how she gets here. I certainly wasn't expecting her at the séance. I've never seen her actually inside the House before. Really, I'm telling you the truth…' I added, pathetically anxious to please – and to avoid another slap.

She eyed me, frowning, as if deciding whether to believe what I had just said. Naturally, I left out the fact that Tatiana had been in my bed later that same night.

'Well then, Nico…' She warmed slightly. 'If you don't *know* any more about her, give me an opinion.'

'Opinion?'

'Yes. What is she like when you talk to her? How does she act: sane, mad, deluded, sensible?'

'Hmm…sane, I suppose, although there is that stuff about being the Tsar's daughter. She seems confident that it's true…'

'Am I to believe, young man, that you have conversations with Her Imperial Highness Tatiana Nicolaevna Romanova who was murdered in Russia in 1918, fifty years ago? Come on, Nicholas, you *will* make me angry if you take me for such a fool!'

I was confused. Before, Madame Lili had been acting as if she herself truly believed that this was fifty years ago and that she needed to meet with Russian soldiers to discuss the Civil War… Before I could reply, she changed completely and, reaching out, rested her hand gently on my cheek. 'Come on, Nico, I thought we were friends. We have been…er…close, haven't we? You see now that I can be a good friend to you. Now, just tell me what you think,' she coaxed. 'I mean, we can't have trespassers tramping all over the House, can we?'

'No, of course not, Madame Lili.'

It crossed my mind to say just 'Lili' but I didn't dare, friends or not. Instead, I tried hard to think of something to say to please her and maintain her change of mood, but to my dismay my mind was steadily going out of focus, and I became terrified that she would learn somehow what I had done with our famous trespasser.

'Very well, Nicholas, perhaps you would be so kind as to keep a special watch for her in future and tell me the minute you have some news?'

It was an order. I was being dismissed. Even her body language was telling me it was time to go.

I'm not sure how I managed to stand up, I was feeling so strange. It was as though I was very drunk but I knew that wasn't the case. I thought of the champagne and the fact that Madame Lili had not drunk any of it herself.

She had to help me to the door. There seemed no question of a goodnight kiss. How I made it to my bedroom is a mystery – one of many in that House.

I fell on to the bed fully clothed but soon sat up in an effort to stop the room spinning. It was inconceivable that I could be so drunk on just two glasses of champagne and, not for the first time, I suspected that I had been drugged. In fact, the more I thought about it, the more certain it seemed. Something was being added to my drinks – my coffee, and particularly the tea that was constantly urged on me from the ever-boiling samovar.

Until I arrived at the House, I had always enjoyed fairly robust health, and at nearly twenty-three years old and on three square meals each day I should have been at my peak…

The spinning must have ceased, because I lay back and eventually fell into a deep sleep.

I awoke in a panic. Sinking back on to the pillow, I retraced as far as I was able the events of the evening before. Had it really happened as I remembered? Did Madame Lili and I make love on the carpet in front of the fire in her salon? Was any of it real? Once before, she had transported me to the vast, snow-covered steppes and I had felt the gleaming sabre smash my skull and it had all seemed so real that I nearly died of fright; an illusion – a brilliant one – but an illusion just the same. Now, to get information from me about Tatiana, it was the iron fist in the velvet glove. Somehow I felt disappointed at those thoughts yet, at the same time, it went easier on my conscience. Perhaps I hadn't cheated on Natalie at all – at least not with Madame Lili. And, if I had been drugged and deluded last night, perhaps the same was true of the night before with Tatiana. Had she really even been in my bed? Was it just another part of some huge illusion that was being practised on me?

But, even as I asked myself these questions, I knew I was just desperately seeking to salve my conscience to avoid the painful truth that I had slept with three women in the same house in as many days, and betrayed the one that I professed to be deeply in love with. If Natalie ever found out, or even suspected, it would have a devastating effect on her health and fragile sanity.

And supposing, just supposing, that I *had* made love to Madame Lili – that it was only partly an illusion – it meant that I had handed her the means to blackmail me, and control me totally.

Disgusted with myself and panicking about the consequences, I dressed and went down to breakfast, hoping to stop these frightening ideas filling my head and with a half-formed thought about handing in my notice and leaving the House before everything came to light.

Amélie looked up as I entered the kitchen, eyeing me closely, her eyebrows forming an unspoken question. I smiled at her and tried to look more relaxed than I felt. She continued to stare at me and finally I felt I had to say something.

'Look, I'm wearing your cross, Amélie. I'm sure it helps keep me from anything untoward.'

'Untoward!' she scoffed. 'Evil, you mean!'

This sudden display of feeling from one usually so quiet and reserved quite surprised me. I poured some coffee and, when I looked up, she was standing so close that it made me jump. Leaning even closer, her face red from the fire, she whispered fiercely, 'Monsieur Nicholas, you must leave this House! You are in danger here! Don't you feel it?' Her baleful eyes bore into mine. 'You must leave now, while you still can.'

There was a noise by the door and she looked up, the fear showing in her face. Then, furtively and even more quietly than before, she whispered, 'This is an ungodly place. These people…'

'Amélie!'

It was Anya, peering round the door.

'Amélie! What *are* you saying?'

When she saw me, she forced a smile as Amélie moved quickly away back to the stove, her face flushing even redder at being caught out. I could see that Anya was angry and when she smiled at me again it was almost a grimace. She was struggling to control her feelings, but, by the time she had crossed the kitchen to take my arm, her features were composed into her habitual serenity.

'Nicholas, join me for breakfast in the library. It's ages since we had a tête-à-tête.'

She turned her face up at me with that look of amusement in her eyes so that I couldn't refuse, and yielded to her gentle tug on my arm.

The library table was set for two, with the dreaded samovar in full swing and blinis with smoked salmon and scrambled eggs. But I wasn't interested in eating, and nor was Anya, it seemed, because, while serving the inevitable black tea, she interrogated me about my meeting with Madame Lili.

'So, what did she do to you, Nico?'

'*Do* to me? Don't you mean *say* to me?'

'You know what I mean. What happened?'

I wondered how much to tell her – whether to confide in her – and decided against the full, unexpurgated version.

'Well…we talked about the séance and, of course, about the girl who appeared there…you know, Tatiana.'

'Yes indeed: and the question is, who the hell is she? She's got us…everybody…running around in circles. This is a very private house. It used to be so secure.'

'Anya, look at me. Hand on heart, I know no more about her than you do…I mean, in terms of hard facts. I saw her in the garden a couple of times, that's all.'

'I bet Madame Lili didn't go for that answer,' she said archly. 'She would have wanted more than that from you. What did she do to you, Nico? Tell me, please.'

I could see there was no getting out of it. This whole scene, the intimate breakfast for two, the 'you can trust me' approach, was carefully contrived to satisfy Anya's curiosity. At least it told me one thing: there seemed to be no complicity between Madame Lili and Anya, otherwise why would she have to ask?

I knew I would have to tell her something – anything that she would believe and let me alone.

'Well you know Madame Lili, Anya. I think she tried to hypnotise me. She certainly got me drunk. But, sorry to disappoint you, that was it really.'

She gave me a hard, old-fashioned look as though she didn't believe a word of it and then, leaning close, whispered, 'Did she try to seduce you, Nico?'

'Certainly not! What do you take me for, Anya?'

I feigned offence. She sat back and shrieked with laughter. 'Why, a fool, of course, Nico. You're a man. You've had the hots for Madame Lili ever since you first met her. The pupils in your eyes go heart-shaped at the mention of her name.'

I felt genuinely offended at that. It didn't seem to me that she was joking. Then she reached out and touched my cheek. 'Don't be sulky with me, Nicolai Feodorovitch. We will always be friends, won't we? And friends may tease each other.'

I was beginning to think that all these 'friends' were rather bad for me and began to search round for an excuse to finish breakfast and leave. Anya must have sensed this, because she stood up, rubbed the back of my head and announced that she had things to do.

'See you at dinner, Nico.'

She smiled a long, slow, complicit smile at me before disappearing round the door.

I finished my tea and, for the first time since coming to the House, began to consider what I would do when I left.

Upstairs in my sitting room, I began to plot my future. The 'mystique' of this House was getting a little too much for me. I felt that, somehow, I was digging a hole that I would, some day soon, fall into. My instincts were telling me, loud and clear, that the walls of this place were closing in around me. The sense of cosiness and security that had earlier so impressed me had changed to a claustrophobic atmosphere where I was no longer able to apply any logic or common sense to what was inexorably being played out around me.

As soon as I could solve the problem of ensuring a future with Natalie, I…we…were going to leave.

CHAPTER 9

# The Invisible Shotgun

*'Youth is easily deceived because it is quick to hope.'*

ARISTOTLE

*D*r Voikin's surgery was not the sort of place you would want to spend much time in. A poky, dreary cubbyhole of a room on the rear first floor landing of the right wing of the House, it had one small window facing on to the rear gardens. The furniture was sparse: an examination couch, a desk and three plain wooden chairs; glass-panelled cabinets lined two walls, their contents either dark bottles of unspecified liquid or stainless steel instruments, dishes and syringes, seemingly designed for horrendously painful purposes. A vague smell of carbolic pervaded the place, mixed with the smell from the desk oil lamp that had to be lit during the day, the place was so gloomy.

Three weeks had passed since the séance and what had followed. To my relief, things had been fairly routine, compared to what had gone before; Natalie had occasionally attended lessons, but more often either been unwell herself or attending the Grand Duchess who was indisposed, a pattern that had become familiar to me. She was warm and affectionate, but did not come again to my bed, and such was my guilt about my betrayal of her that I didn't press the matter, although I loved her more and more.

Then I had been summoned, completely unexpectedly, by Anya, who admitted that she had no knowledge of the purpose of the meeting except that Maître Chermakov would also be present.

Dr Voikin was alone when I arrived. He looked uncomfortable in his high butterfly collar and, as he stood up to greet me, an odour of mothballs and cigarettes wafted off his clothes. Again, I was struck by how much he resembled photographs that I had seen of Dr Crippen at the time of his arrest.

Maître Chermakov walked in just behind me, his thin, dark, obviously dyed hair slicked down with brilliantine, a stark contrast to his parchment-like skin and hollow cheeks. When he spoke, his face resembled a skull and his mouth a steel trap. With his black clothes, he looked like an undertaker.

We all sat down and, with no pretence at small talk or the niceties of social conversation, Chermakov gestured peremptorily at Voikin to begin.

The good doctor shifted uncomfortably on his chair and nervously cleared his throat. I guessed something serious was coming and his uneasiness communicated itself to all of us.

'Er…um…*monsieur*, you are, I'm sure, aware that the Princess…er…Natalya, suffers from a…er…chronic neurosis?' Not waiting for me to answer, he continued, 'This being a form of *petit mal*, you might say, verging perhaps, it may be said, on paranoia, er…eclectic in nature and, er…episodic…'

'Spare us the medical jargon, Voikin,' Chermakov cut in petulantly. 'Just get to the reason we're here!'

Voikin eyed him nervously before continuing. 'Well, anyway, it…er…has been ascertained during a routine examination… er…that her Imperial Highness…'

'For God's sake man!' Chermakov exploded. 'Tell him!'

Voikin flushed crimson and croaked, 'The Princess is in the very early stages of…'

'She's pregnant!' Chermakov shouted, totally exasperated.

There followed a long silence as the two men stared at me, trying to gauge my reaction. Reaction, though, was too weak a word – paralysis would have been a more apt description.

'Pregnant.' I repeated the word aloud, as though I couldn't understand what it meant. Slowly, the meaning sank in. My mouth went dry and I swallowed hard. What reply did they expect from me? What reply *could* I make? After what seemed an age, I heard myself saying, 'Of course, I accept total responsibility for the situation…'

'Situation?' Chermakov exploded again. 'Do you hear him, Voikin? He calls it a "situation"!' His sallow complexion had turned a livid crimson and he thrust his face close to mine. 'This is not a "situation", *monsieur*, this is a crime! You have committed a serious criminal offence!'

Now, I accepted that I had been totally irresponsible, and knew that, as a tutor, I had seriously betrayed my position of trust, and I didn't feel in the least proud of myself, but to say it was a criminal offence was, I thought, a bit exaggerated. Suddenly feeling bolder, I parried back at Chermakov.

'Natalie is no longer a child. She is almost eighteen years old – well over the age of consent, and a young woman who knows her own mind. Unfortunate and irresponsible on my part it may well have been, but criminal it is not. It takes two to tango, *maître*.'

As soon as I said this, I realised that such a flippant comment was totally out of place. But I couldn't think how else to put it. Chermakov quickly withdrew his face, as if he'd been burned. His pointing finger came up to replace it and his eyes narrowed to slits.

'*Monsieur,*' he said quietly. 'The law and its application is my profession. I do not use words lightly.' His eyes opened wide and fixed on mine, like a snake hypnotising a rabbit. 'Allow me to explain…' he whispered patronisingly. 'The Princess Natalya suffers from a chronic, sometimes serious, mental illness. That, at least, you are able to understand?'

I nodded.

'As a result of this, she has been…how do you say… "sectioned", according to French mental health regulations and legislation. This means, *monsieur,* in layman's terms, that she has been certified insane and confined to this House. Do you understand that?'

Though shocked, I nodded hesitantly and he, sensing my dismay, closed in for the kill.

'Now, although we live very privately here in this House, we are nonetheless governed by the French Penal Code. According to this country's mental health laws, any person certified insane is deemed *not* to be competent to give consent. Do you understand, *monsieur?* Natalya cannot give consent!'

He paused for that to penetrate my humble, non-legal brain.

'Therefore, according to law, any sexual intercourse that has taken place between you was, on her part, non-consensual. Think about that carefully, *monsieur.* And, if a sex act is non-consensual, it is called *rape!*' he shouted triumphantly.

I felt a rising nausea and mumbled, 'But how was I to know she was…er…certified?'

'Oh, *monsieur,*' Chermakov gloated, sensing complete victory. 'Oh, *monsieur,* ignorance is not a defence in French law. You raped her; it's as simple as that.'

I felt sick to my stomach. Part of me was thinking 'ridiculous' and the other part was starting to comprehend that Chermakov was right. The wicked tutor taking advantage of his mentally ill pupil; I could see the headlines. Panic rose up in me, and under the table my knees started to tremble. Chermakov leaned back in triumph, disdain and disgust written all over his face, and little sympathy came from Dr Voikin, who just sat nodding slowly, showing his complete agreement with all that his colleague had said.

There followed a long silence punctuated only by Chermakov lighting a particularly odorous Russian cigarette.

The moments ticked by, registered by the clock on Voikin's desk. Finally, not trusting myself to speak without my voice breaking, I looked up at Chermakov with what I hoped was a look of contrition but was probably one of complete defeat. Eventually, I managed to say, 'Can you advise me, *maître?*'

My complete surrender seemed to work wonders on him. He made a steeple with his fingers.

'Well, there *is* a solution, albeit a partial one. He leaned back and let his words hang in the air, deliberately prolonging my anguish. 'Of course, the Princess is expecting your child and nothing can change that. In fact, it rather compounds the criminality of your relationship. However…' Again he paused, enjoying seeing me squirm. 'However, were you to be *married*…'

'But how can she consent to marriage?' I cut in, desperately grasping at any possible way out.

'She cannot, *monsieur*, but her legal guardian, the Grand Duchess, could.'

'But, under French law…' I broke off miserably, looking at my feet.

Chermakov continued, 'Such a marriage would be a private affair, in this House, sanctified by the Russian Orthodox Church. If the Duchess recognises this and is, of course, prepared to agree to it, we would dispense with the civil marriage required by the French State.'

'But the "rape"…would the police –?'

'The police will have nothing to do with it if we do not report it,' he cut in. 'If you agree to the marriage, I shall – though reluctantly I must say – recommend to the Grand Duchess that the police should not be informed.'

I looked up and he read the relief in my face.

'There will, of course, be conditions, *monsieur*, with which you will be required to abide.'

'Of course,' I gasped.

'That's settled, then. I will draw up a deed of marriage, including all the conditions, and submit it to the Grand Duchess to approve.' He got up from the table. At the door, he turned, 'And you, *monsieur*, had better pray that she does.'

Under the lime trees, my favourite bench in the rose arbour should have reminded me of the beautiful spring day. But it could not; my mind was far away, churning on the meeting with Voikin and Chermakov.

I was scared. What they had said amounted to blackmail, pure and simple. There was no other way to describe it – nasty, threatening, vindictive blackmail. Yet I knew what they said was true. I had done something very stupid and irresponsible and I could go to prison for it. The thought terrified me. They had only to report me to the police to ensure my downfall. I couldn't run, I had nowhere to go, and I couldn't hide because without papers I would be picked up within hours. I had no money and no one to help me.

Then there was Natalie. How must she be feeling? Did Voikin tell her she was pregnant or did she just know herself? Had they even told her? Did she *want* to marry me? Had she thought that somehow I could save her, help her escape from this House where she had been a prisoner all her life? But I couldn't even help myself.

The more I thought it through, the more I realised what a fool I had been. I had fallen right into their trap: a honey trap. I was now convinced that I'd been set up, and it all seemed so obvious now. They must have known that, sooner or later, like most young women, Natalie would want her independence. She could not survive outside this House, so her future life must be brought here to her – a future including a husband and a family but all within the confines of this House; a life in shadows in a House of shadows.

The advertisement for a tutor, the insistence on my living in, of contracting out of any existence exterior to this place…all of it had clearly been contrived with one aim in mind.

I poured a glass of burgundy from the bottle I'd liberated from the pantry and settled back on the bench, trying to get a grip. Everything – the clouds, the birds, the flowers – carried on, regardless of my complete and utter turmoil.

Then, as if in answer to my thoughts, there was Natalie, standing in front of me, beautiful, smiling and serene. She sat down beside me, took my hand and put her head on my shoulder.

'Be calm, Nicholas. Everything is going to be all right. We love each other, don't we? We want to be together. This way, we will be married and be together always.' Then she sat up. 'That *is* what you want, Nico, isn't it?' she asked, her eyes full of anxiety.

My heart went out to her. I wondered how she could possibly want anything to do with a selfish idiot like me.

'Of course it's what I want,' I reassured her, and slowly, as I said it, I realised that it was true. What I had considered a trap might actually be a doorway to getting what I wanted. I wanted this girl, princess or not, ill or not, and I wanted to spend my life with her, wherever she was, and for her to have my child – our child. Why was I so anxious for the future? She was going to be my wife, and so what if we were trapped in this House? It could not be forever. When the Grand Duchess died, Natalie would surely inherit. Maybe, in the interim, medical science would discover a cure for her illness. Maybe, one day, we could be free of this House – and maybe then we wouldn't want to leave!

Natalie was still staring at me, concern written all over her lovely face. 'Nico, you do want to marry me, don't you? Please tell me you do.'

'More than I can say!'

She pressed her face against mine and I felt her tears and the sobs racking her slender body. We stayed like that a long while and, when at last she stood up, she was smiling. 'Walk with me, Nico, and I'll explain what's going to happen.'

I scarcely remember everything she told me then. She rattled it all off so quickly and with obvious pleasure. I gathered that I was to be elevated to the nobility, given a title by the Grand Duchess so as to avoid a 'morganatic' marriage and introducing a commoner into the family. It appeared that the Grand Duchess was on good terms with His Imperial Highness Vladimir, the Tsar in exile, and he would make the title official. We were to be married here at the House by Father Feodor in an Orthodox ceremony, with me using the name 'Nicolai'. Several rooms on the third floor would be made available to us, converted into an apartment. The baby would be born at home and looked after by a nanny and…

…*and we will all live happily ever after*, I thought, with bad grace.

In the meantime, the Grand Duchess would be donating a ring for our engagement, a family heirloom of great value. I was formally, in writing, to ask for Natalya's hand in marriage, and an engagement party would follow. The wedding would take place in a week's time.

Then, smiling happily, Natalie went off back to the House to arrange the making of her wedding dress.

Back on my bench, I was having a severe attack of reality. Engagement, elevation to the nobility, marriage, fatherhood, happy families… I looked at the nearest rose bush and tried to concentrate on something 'normal'.

I reached out and picked a rose, pricking my hand in the process. Inhaling the fragrance, I watched the blood trickle down my fingers and managed to regain some self-control. To possess something of beauty, I thought, you had to suffer in some way. What an irony that I should have been studying Sartre, Bergson and Camus and yet be living a life more 'existential' than any of them ever dreamt about.

It seemed as though my entire existence up to this point had been dull and commonplace and now I had suddenly come alive in this strange place, though I wasn't absolutely sure yet that I liked the change, or that 'alive' was the correct description. The House seemed to represent the victory of death over life, the old over the new, and obscurity over reason.

And yet somehow the fact that I was being blackmailed into a shotgun marriage no longer mattered to me now. I really felt that I had won. After all, I had the hand in marriage of the girl I adored and, to be brutally honest for once, the only person I had ever loved more than myself! A life of total selfishness was about to change.

Nor did the thought of being a father intimidate me. We would have a comfortable home in this House, in Paris, with servants to look after us and, almost certainly, some sort of financial allowance from the Grand Duchess. How could I possibly have afforded all that as a penniless, unqualified student, homeless and without even residential status or a student visa? If we had been able to leave as I had originally hoped and imagined, could Natalie have ever survived the life I would have inflicted on her? In truth, the more I thought it all through, the more it seemed a wonderful solution to all my problems. When the Grand Duchess died, as she probably would quite soon, I would surely become my wife's legal guardian and then, slowly at first, we would change our lives. I would start to take Natalie on short trips away from the House, gradually introduce her to a wider society…modern life…

I stopped. She was so beautiful but so very fragile; to impose my values on her would be to break her in every respect. And anyway, what *were* my values? I had been quick to criticise this House with its Victorian way of life, but what could modern Paris offer in its place: riots, unrest, instability, a frantic lifestyle full of violence and stress, with money at the centre of all ambition?

I had come full circle. Now I was happy to marry, happy to stay, happy to opt out of the modern world for a life of love and affection.

Another glass of wine compounded my newfound optimism and I had just decided to finish the bottle when a slight movement caught my eye. Sitting opposite, staring at me, was Tatiana. Though I recognised her immediately, I couldn't prevent an involuntary start, and spilled some of the wine on my shoes.

'Clumsy boy!' she chided me, smiling.

'Oh, Tatiana! How do you do that?'

'Do what, Nicolai Feodorovitch?'

'Just appear like that. Just a moment ago that was an empty chair.'

'I've been here for some time, Nicholas, but you see me only when you want to. You must learn to look at the spaces in between,' she said, mysteriously. 'Please not to be angry. I thought you might be pleased I am here. You seem so distracted of late.' She eyed me anxiously.

Now whether it was my newfound euphoria at being about to marry Natalya or the effect of the wine on my precarious grip on reality, I can't be sure, but I suddenly decided to solve the Tatiana 'phenomenon' once and for all, and start my new life without any questions and mysteries.

I realised that I had never really *looked* at Tatiana. Of course, I'd seen her several times, but I couldn't recall actually studying her, so to speak. She seemed to appear always when some crisis was distracting me.

She sat across the table from me, a matter of a few feet away, and in spite of the effects of the wine I could see her very clearly in the bright sunshine. As I had first thought, she appeared to be about nineteen or twenty years old, although her Victorian-style clothing and hair made her seem older. Tall and slim, she had great elegance and poise, and there was definitely something regal in the way she held herself; an 'aristocratic bearing' that was reflected in the way she held her head high on her slender neck and even the way she composed her features. Like Natalie, she had a fine, slender nose and a small but sensuous mouth and even teeth of a slightly greyish white. Her most striking features were her high cheekbones, which made her blue-grey eyes look smaller, as if she were squinting into the sun. Her auburn hair was piled loosely on top of her head in a way I associated with the same period as her clothes. As far as I could tell, she wore no make-up except the 'bloom' of her youth.

'Who *are* you, Tatiana? …I mean, really? I know you already told me you are the second daughter of Nicholas, Tsar of all the Russias, but who are you really?'

'Who do you want me to be?' she asked, the smile gone.

'I don't know. The girl who lives next door, perhaps...a secret friend of Natalya's...a local amateur actress...'

'An actress!' she shouted at me, her eyes flashing angrily. 'Is that what you think, *monsieur* – that I look like an *actress*?'

She was genuinely annoyed and I regretted immediately saying such a thing and tried to back-pedal to calm her growing anger.

'No, of course not, Tatiana. I'm sorry. I expressed myself badly. I certainly didn't mean to insult you. It's just that everybody keeps asking me about you. You seem to have caused a panic in the entire household. I just wanted to learn a bit more about you, where you live...and how you get into this garden...the gates are always locked...and how you were in that room when we had the famous séance...'

'Séance?' She frowned her puzzlement. After a long pause, she leaned forward, as if about to impart a huge secret, and whispered, 'We are the Old Ones. We live in the spaces in between.'

'I'm sorry for being so dense, Tatiana, but I don't understand. In between what?'

She leaned back and looked at me, but made no attempt at any further answers. We just sat and looked at each other. Now I had studied her close up, so to speak, I decided that she was indeed very beautiful. She was a person of contradictions, slim and elegant, haughty yet warm and gentle, serious yet naïve, mature yet sometimes childlike.

The sun had dropped low in the sky and now shone directly on us with a warm, golden glow. The wine, the warmth of the sunlight, my emotional exhaustion, all conspired against me, and for just a moment I must have closed my eyes.

'Nicholas!'

I started awake. The seat opposite me was now empty – Tatiana had, once again, disappeared. Almost immediately, Madame Lili appeared; it had been her voice that had called me. 'With whom were you speaking, Nicholas?' she demanded sharply in her precise French.

'Er, no one,' I replied stupidly, trying to avoid the inevitable third degree that I knew would follow if I mentioned Tatiana.

She came very close to me as I stood up for her, her lips pursed over her beautiful teeth, in a familiar gesture that seemed to signify anger.

'Nicolai Feodorovitch.' She almost spat the words. 'You seem always to have a perverse desire to lie to me.'

Before I could reply, she slapped me so hard across the face that I flinched back out of range, hardly believing she could do such a thing to me again.

'I ask you again, *monsieur*. You do not talk to yourself. Who was with you just now?' She leaned closer, her deep voice reinforcing the threat. 'Do *not* try to deceive me again!'

'Tatiana,' I blurted out. 'It was Tatiana.'

Madame Lili sighed deeply, sat down uncomfortably close to me and remained silent for several minutes, then looking me straight in the eyes, said quietly, 'You know, Nicholas, one could be tempted to believe that this Tatiana is a figment of your imagination.'

I thought that a strange thing to say, given that she had seen her at the séance, and I said as much. She confined her reply to a grunt of disgust and continued to stare out across the garden as if looking for someone.

I waited patiently to see how the situation would develop, surprised at how easily the woman intimidated me. I wondered whether, now that she seemed to have calmed down, she would offer some sort of apology for striking me. But I waited in vain.

'Yes, it doesn't make sense,' she murmured, seemingly to herself, and then turned to me again and asked, 'Who *is* she, *monsieur*?'

It was the first time that she had addressed me so formally and an obvious sign of her continuing displeasure. Anxious to defuse this growing tendency for violence on her part, I tried to avoid any trace of flippancy in my voice. 'She said she was one of the "Old Ones", whatever that means.'

'And do you believe her?' she asked flatly, staring at me intently.

'Well, er…I don't really understand what she meant by it. I mean, the family…the Tsar and his family…are all dead, murdered by the Bolsheviks in 1918…'

'In the House of Special Purpose,' she said slowly, enunciating every word and staring unblinking into my eyes in a way that made me feel very uneasy. Not knowing what on earth I was rambling on about or what to say next, I just nodded. She said nothing more, and the silence grew so uncomfortable that I felt obliged to continue.

'She does seem to know a great deal about the Imperial Family, though – and she really does look incredibly like the photos of the Grand Duchess Tatiana in the books in the library…'

My voice trailed off as I noticed a frown disfigure Madame Lili's lovely face. She was more uneasy and disturbed than I had ever seen her before. Always in control, she now looked drawn and ill at ease, and I cast around for something to say to take advantage of her unwonted vulnerability. Before I could say manage it, she sat up and asked, 'How do you summon her?'

'I don't. She just appears.'

'But always to *you*,' she said with a sneer.

'It seems so, yes.'

'Have you ever touched her, Nicholas?'

I felt a trap opening and to give myself time to think, repeated her question. 'Touched her?'

Madame Lili sighed her impatience. 'Held her hand? Kissed her?'

'We held hands at the séance,' I offered, pleased at my smart answer and at the same time avoiding any mention of things more intimate.

'And does she question you about us?' She nodded her head towards the House.

'No, never, Madame Lili.'

My answers seemed to reassure her a little and her frown relaxed. After a moment, she got up to go. I struggled to stand, the effect of the wine weighing heavily upon me. She turned towards the House but then turned back to me, reached out and gently touched my face where she had slapped me. She said nothing but offered a slight smile, which I took to be an apology of sorts. I watched her long, dark shadow glide towards the House as the sun set blood-red behind her.

I missed Tatiana then: a free spirit to talk to when everyone else seemed to have a hidden agenda, following some carefully laid plan. Nothing in the House was what it seemed. Nothing happened there that was spontaneous; everything was pre-planned. I hadn't just stumbled into this House by accident, I realised that now. This whole scenario was carefully staged. Obviously, Natalie's needs needed to be addressed and, for whatever reason, it had to be me.

For weeks I had been tricked, deceived, drugged, hypnotised and now slapped and threatened with prison. How had it come to this? Why had I not left as soon as it had started to become unpleasant? Just walked out? If I stayed, it would continue, but now I would be with Natalie and under her protection. Who knew: I might even turn the tables on them all – exert a little moral blackmail of my own.

In the meantime, I needed to talk to someone I could trust. I willed Tatiana to reappear and waited in vain. What and where were these 'spaces in between' that she mentioned?

Now that the euphoria of the wine was wearing off, a hint of depression was edging in and the sunshine was fading fast. I still felt drunk and closed my eyes again, only to hear a soft footfall on the path. For a moment, I thought Tatiana was back. But it was Anya. I suppose my disappointment must have shown in my face, because she greeted me with an attempt at a smile that failed miserably.

'Madame Lili thought you might need some coffee,' she said flatly, putting down the coffee pot just a little too hard. She poured me a cup, but not one for herself. The implication was that I was the one who was drunk. She sighed and plonked herself down opposite me.

There had been a time when Anya and I had been close – friends, that is, or at least so I thought. When I had first met her, she had been so nice to me, in a sisterly sort of way. We were both misfits, neither family nor servants, and we had had a kind of complicity, an unspoken agreement that we would look after each other. I had trusted her when I found I could trust no one else. That now seemed a long while ago. It was very clear which side Anya was on now, and I no longer trusted her at all. Exactly when this change had occurred was difficult to say, though it seemed that she had cooled towards me after Tatiana's appearance holding my hand at the séance. I suppose I couldn't blame her. She was, after all, part of the House. As the English say, she knew which side her bread was buttered.

This afternoon she seemed almost hostile, probably because she had found out what I had done to Natalie. She just sat there considering me, with a look of disdain. I felt dismayed by this. She had been my last refuge in the House, and without her support I would now be totally isolated. Of course, there was Tatiana, but she was nebulous, ethereal, out of reach, without any means of contact, and, very possibly, quite mad. I tried, clumsily, to mend some bridges.

'How are you, Anya? Long time no see…'

She was having none of it. 'You so disappoint me, Nicolai Feodorovitch – so smug, so confident and yet such a fool, outwitted every step of the way…'

Her eyes narrowed and she almost spat the words. For the first time in a long while, she used '*vous*' instead of '*tu*', and the new formality was not lost on me. Unprepared for that level of hostility, I cast around for something expiatory to say. But she had not finished with me yet.

'Just look at you,' she continued relentlessly. 'Drunk again! You just don't get it, do you? Everything you do here is manipulated by others. You've behaved like a tomcat in a cattery. I must be the only one you haven't fornicated with!'

So *that* was it! She knew what I'd been up to and she felt neglected, scorned, and a woman scorned... I heard myself saying, 'Oh, *that*! Well, it's not too late...'

I heard myself saying it but was powerless to stop. It was an outrageous, unforgivable thing to say. She jumped up and, for a moment, I thought I was going to get the hot coffee thrown in my face. I would have deserved it. But she stopped suddenly and her contorted features gradually relaxed into a smile belied by the fire in her eyes and I knew instinctively that I had made a dangerous enemy out of a caring friend.

Unable to think of anything to say to redeem myself, I watched as she slowly reached for a cup and poured me a thick black coffee. Still not sure whether it would be thrown in my face, I reached out and accepted it warily. Anya sat down and watched me with a look that seemed to say, *I'm smiling now but I will settle with you when the time is right.* I could only hope to fall into the hole that I had stupidly dug for myself and wake up on another planet.

Even as I sipped the coffee, I knew I was making a big mistake. Accepting any sort of a drink in this House was to invite the unknown. But I just didn't care any more.

I had not long to wait. Within moments, whatever had been put into the coffee began to take effect. Though the afternoon sun was weakening towards evening, it seemed suddenly very bright, dazzlingly bright, and the roses around me took on an amazingly colourful hue and the leaves jumped into a fluorescent green, while the ground seemed to drop beneath my feet.

Almost as quickly as this beautiful kaleidoscope appeared, it began to fade into ugly dark patterns that somehow seemed full of menace and danger, reaching out to drag me down.

I looked across at Anya, a mute appeal for help, only to receive a sneer and then a look of pure malevolence; then, as I looked at her, her face metamorphosed into a leering, fleshless skull. I gripped the edge of the table and closed my eyes, fighting the onset of whatever drug had been in the drink. But it did no good! Even with my eyes tightly shut, I continued to see Anya's face turn into a skull, the black eye sockets and the rictus of the clenched teeth leering ever closer to my face. In an effort to escape I struggled to my feet, knocking over the table, coffee pot and chair. Staggering, I lurched towards the House, trying not to look back at the hideous face I knew was right behind me. The last thing I can remember was Serge gripping me tightly while Anya laughed in my face…

Even sleep couldn't save me from the terrors of that 'trip', and I awoke next day feeling totally drained and very miserable. The House and its denizens carried on as normal – if, indeed, 'normal' is the right word – and moved around me as though I had become invisible; I passed what was left of the morning wandering about the many rooms and in and out of the gardens without seeing anyone who wanted to talk. How I longed to see Natalya or, perhaps, Tatiana, but no one came.

Whatever had been put into my coffee the afternoon before eventually wore off. I decided not to confront Anya about it – after all, I considered I deserved to be punished for the way I had behaved towards her. I decided to treat it as a warning – as if one were necessary after all this time – and avoid any food or drink that was not being served to others.

Perhaps now that they had achieved their purpose, of finding a suitor for Natalya, and had the situation completely under their control, they would leave me alone and concentrate on the engagement event. I call it an event because, if I had expected a party – I mean festivities of some sort – I would have been seriously disappointed.

## CHAPTER 10

# The Wedding

*'So you will be delivered from the forbidden woman, from the foreign woman with her smooth words, who forsakes the companion of her youth and forgets the covenant of her God; for her house sinks down to death and her paths to the departed; none who go to her come back, nor do they regain the paths of life.'*

PROVERBS 2:16–19

Something had definitely changed in the House. Of course, with the coming of summer it was bound to be different; without the dark nights, coal fires and the constant use of oil lamps and candles, the cosiness had gone out of it.

But there was a different change – a change of atmosphere. In some indefinable way, the House had taken on the different attitude of its people. Since the recent events, relationships seemed to have altered; a subtle, almost indefinable change, but a change nonetheless.

The evenings spent round the kitchen fire were no longer so welcoming. Something in the demeanour of the others was just not the same, making them less approachable, less relaxed around me. They no longer seemed to know how to address me in a relaxed and familiar way. I was no longer one of them and now belonged, they clearly thought, 'upstairs'. Of course, no one actually said that, but it was clear to me that I was in No Man's Land, too posh for the servants and not posh enough for the masters. To some extent, I suppose I felt the same. How could the fiancé of a princess be seen to get drunk with the 'staff'?

Yet I missed them. I could not imagine any sort of social intercourse with the likes of Chermakov and Voikin, nor was I invited to join Madame Lili and the Grand Duchess, and even Natalya seemed too busy to spend much time with me. Only Anya sought me out, and that was merely to discuss plans for the wedding. Her attitude was cold and businesslike. My appalling behaviour and the episode with the drugged coffee was never mentioned, and I felt that Anya's revenge was far from over.

I found myself wishing for the good old days of flirting with Natalie during her lessons. For the first time in many weeks, I thought of my old life in Paris. My mind left out the miserable bits and, conveniently, recalled only the good times. The city must be back to normal by now, bearing, no doubt, some scars from the riots, and the Left's constant obsession with yet another revolution, sated for a few decades. The Sorbonne would be open for lectures again and the nearby cafés thriving and alive with the pseudo-academic conversations that students need to bolster their 'intellectual' image.

What had become of Bruno, Aurélie and Max? Was it business as usual at the café, with Jean-Marie serving endless croissants and coffees, while moaning that the students never left tips? What would they make of all this, my friends? Me marrying a Russian princess! I could hardly believe it myself. Nostalgia for my student life rolled over me.

Still, you can't go back, can you? As my mother used to say: 'You've made your bed and now you must lie in it.'

It seemed that the protocol for Russian engagements was very different from that of Western Europe, at least among the aristocracy in general and this House in particular.

It took the form of a sort of garden party, with a long trestle table brought out to the big lawn at the front of the House, carefully laid with silverware, white linen and glass. Drinks – mainly Russian champagne – were served at about 3pm, accompanied by blinis with smoked salmon or caviar.

The food was excellent and everyone was there. Despite the warm, sunny weather, all the men wore dark suits and ties, except for Sergei, who again wore his new *rubashka* and long Cossack coat open at the front to reveal his cartridge belt and dagger. Chermakov even sported an ancient butterfly collar and a suit that reeked of camphor and mothballs.

All the women wore long dresses, even the maids and Amélie the cook, who for a day appeared to be guests rather than staff. Of course, Natalya and Madame Lili stole the show. In contrast to the sombre men's suits, the women wore long white dresses pulled in at the waist and with high collars and jewels on a black ribbon at their throats. Natalya wore dainty, light blue satin shoes, while Madame Lili appeared to be wearing white patent leather, high-buttoned boots. Both carried white parasols, and Madame Lili wore long-sleeved white gloves. Natalie's arms were bare, showing her hands and the diamond engagement ring which I was supposed to have given her.

While she was talking excitedly with Anya and Madame Lili, I took a seat next to Serge, or 'Sergei' as I felt I should call him that day. Resplendent in his uniform, he was nevertheless more relaxed than I had ever seen him. He sat back, smoking his black Russian Balkan Sobranie tobacco, and seemed to be taking a well-earned rest. He didn't speak, but sighed contentedly like a man contemplating the completion of a job well done. He was not alone in that – all the 'staff' seemed to be unusually laid-back. All pretence of formality had gone, and the social barriers dividing the inmates of the House seemed to have broken down in the face of a state of general wellbeing, as though a great and difficult task had been accomplished.

It suddenly dawned on me that that was actually the case… the betrothal of Natalya had been achieved. Such had been the plan all along. I was merely the 'fall guy', the dupe who had fallen for the whole scheme, and now they were all part of the same celebration of a job well done. Each had played his or her part to perfection, and tomorrow the wedding would be their crowning achievement.

But still I didn't actually care! I didn't care that I had been set up. I didn't care that I had been blackmailed and threatened and I didn't care that I had been drugged, hypnotised, deceived and even physically abused because, in my mind, I believed that I had won – I was getting the girl of my dreams and, in so doing, I would eventually be controlling the situation. I didn't listen to that little voice that was telling me, 'You are too clever by half, Nicholas!'

The most dangerous lies are the lies we tell ourselves.

Towards late afternoon, when the shadows on the lawn were long and thin and the sun reduced to dark red, low on the horizon, Madame Lili came to me. No warm familiarity there, no pretence at the newfound easiness of the others. Madame Lili held herself as aloof as on the first day we met. Her only concession to the relaxed tone of the afternoon was to lift the veil of her hat. The dark eyes bored into mine, and the slow smile seemed forced and insincere.

'My dear Nicholas,' she murmured in her deep, husky voice, reaching out her gloved hand for me to kiss. I stood up and, since she made no move to continue, offered her a chair, catching the familiar heavy fragrance of her perfume as she sat down. 'Nicholas, we need to go over a few points about tomorrow – the wedding ceremony…'

She looked away, as if ordering things in her head. I took advantage of her averted gaze to study her closely and realised I had been wrong. Though very formal, she seemed relaxed in herself, with a certain serenity in her eyes, as if infected by the quiet contentment shown by the others scattered around us at the other tables. She seemed almost reluctant to speak on this breathless summer night. She sighed her contentment, her lips parted slightly to show her clenched teeth in a gesture so similar to Natalie's that I wondered yet again if they were related.

Slowly, she reached up and unpinned her hat, her long, thick, dark hair cascading immediately from it. She shook  her head from side to side and wafted her perfume on to the still warm air. In spite of myself, I felt a slow arousal; my eyes fixed on her slender body and I recalled vividly those urgent, intimate moments we had spent, locked together like two animals on heat. Had it really happened? Had I made love to Madame Lili in her boudoir, that night? Or was it, like so much I had experienced in this House, a carefully choreographed scene, an illusion, planted on me, suggested to me, using hypnotism and drugs. I liked to think otherwise.

Whatever it had been then, she aroused me now. Certainly it was not the deep love and affection I felt for Natalie, but a purely physical desire, lust arising from who knows what primordial animal instinct not well connected with acceptable behaviour.

Madame Lili looked up suddenly and stared me straight in the face.

'Do you think, *monsieur*, such thoughts are becoming in one so recently betrothed?'

I could feel myself blushing. Could she really read my thoughts, or had some involuntary movement or expression on my part given the game away?

She jumped up and stood in front of me and I flinched back, fearing at least a slap. Instead she just stared at me, a half-smile verging on a sneer forming on her beautiful face. Then, just as quickly, her body and features relaxed. Her shoulders began to twitch and I realised to my complete bewilderment that she was laughing; it was suppressed and silent, but it was laughter. She recovered immediately and, bending close to my ear, whispered with scarcely concealed contempt, 'Oh, Nicolai Feodorovitch, do not be afraid! All your troubles will soon be over!'

She sat down and looked out across the gardens, which were barely visible in the fading light.

'Now, about the wedding. Listen carefully, Nicholas.'

Barely seeming interested herself, she rattled out some details about the ceremony. I tried hard to concentrate; this was my last hurdle to happiness.

She started with the *svideteli* or witnesses. Serge was to be my best man, Anya would be the matron of honour and she, Madame Lili, Natalie's official guardian in the Grand Duchess's stead, would give the bride away. Father Feodor would perform a rather abbreviated Russian Orthodox ceremony in French (known in Russia as *venchanie*) and the wedding celebrations would take place that night.

She also mentioned something about gold rings being exchanged and some glass-smashing. She added more about candles and wearing crowns but by that time I was having trouble taking it all in. She, too, seemed anxious to be done with it, as if she accepted that it was all a sham – but a necessary sham, especially where Natalya was concerned.

Of course, I was more interested in the *noces* (honeymoon) part of it. I had not made love to Natalie for weeks and my body ached for her.

No mention was made of this, however, and my tentative questions about 'after the wedding' were brushed aside, as though no one had considered that far ahead. Obviously, we would not be going away!

There were other questions I needed to have answered: where exactly was this 'apartment' on the third floor in which we were supposed to live? When was our baby due to be born? What if there were problems with Natalie's health during the pregnancy? Voikin was no obstetrician, nor did he seem much of a doctor.

To all these questions, Madame Lili sighed and said only, 'Be patient, Nicholas; all in the fullness of time. Soon, very soon, such trivia will no longer concern you.'

Her smile very nearly slipped into a sneer again, and I realised, with dismay, what utter contempt she really felt for me. She stood up and, not waiting for me to stand too, said, 'Good evening, Nicholas,' and walked off towards the House, as much an enigma to me then as on the first day we met.

The others had drifted away. I looked around for Natalie but she too had gone, leaving me for company only the lengthening shadows of the dying sun.

So this was it: the eve of my wedding day and it was nothing like I'd imagined it would be. Not that I'd thought much about marriage before. Here, in the heart of a big city, I felt totally isolated, with no way to contact my family or even my friends.

What would they make of such a fantastic tale? When would I even get to tell them about it all and, even if I did, would they believe it?

I looked about me; it was almost completely dark now. Darkness is a lonely place.

The wedding day fell on a Saturday and at 10 a.m., suitably dressed in my dark suit (there had been talk of a uniform but, thankfully, they couldn't find one) and accompanied by an equally suited and booted Sergei, I presented myself to be married in the great dining room of the House.

Father Feodor, who in his Russian Orthodox robes reminded me of a diminutive Archbishop Makarios, was already standing in front of a small table covered with rose-coloured fabric. He lit two candles and, when Natalie joined us, handed a candle to each of us. Natalie was stunning in a white, close-fitting, full-length wedding gown, her face, unfortunately, hidden by a delicate veil. Madame Lili had apparently been persuaded to change her usual black apparel and wore a long, plum-coloured dress. She too was veiled, but her perfume would have marked her out anywhere. The Grand Duchess, it seemed, was too ill to attend.

At a signal from Father Feodor, we advanced to the table. He looked nervous, even furtive, and appeared to be swallowing hard. I noticed that he had written prompts, concealed inside the cover of his prayer book. With a quivering voice, he intoned what I took to be a blessing bestowed upon each of us, and then turned to bless the two gold rings lying on the small table. Then, choosing the smallest ring, he placed it on the second finger of Natalie's right hand and then the other on mine. It was so loose that I had to grip my fingers together to stop it falling off. He then offered up more prayers.

At this point, the *svideteli* entered the room, along with the rest of the wedding guests. Everyone was there, including the kitchen staff and, of course, Anya, who looked very chic in a peach-coloured dress.

I gathered that the placing of rings was symbolic of betrothal but the 'sign' of marriage was yet to come.

After that, Natalie and I walked around the room to another table. Here, two symbolic crowns were blessed and Serge and Madame Lili held them above our heads as we paraded three times round the room, Father Feodor muttering some sort of litany as we went, and awkwardly holding his stole over our joined hands until we arrived at the table holding the Gospel Book. After reading a short verse from this book in heavily accented French, Father Feodor handed us each a glass of wine, which I tried not to gulp down and which Natalie sipped primly, lifting her veil.

She looked radiant. My heart was beating frantically in my chest as I realised that this stunning girl was now my wife.

The service finished, the guests applauded us. Serge, surprisingly, embraced me with a bear hug, and even Voikin and the hateful Chermakov managed to shake my hand, with grimaces that passed for smiles. Madame Lili, her veil finally lifted, gave me a sort of mandatory peck on the cheek and immediately turned away, while Anya's kiss was equally cold and formal. I didn't care. Nothing was going to spoil my happiness that morning, and I held Natalie's hand in a way that I hoped reassured her that she was the most precious thing in my life.

Vodka was produced for Natalie and for me, but I made to refuse it until Serge explained that it was part of the ceremony. Natalie had to drink it too, so I reasoned that it was safe. The toast was to the bride and groom.

'*Cul sec*,' Serge shouted, 'down in one,' and we both complied. It was only a small amount and quite weak by Serge's standards, but the best part was to follow; all the guests began to shout, '*Gorko, Gorko, Gorko!*' *Gorko* means bitter; it was the signal for the bride and bridegroom to kiss for a long time, to take away the bitter taste.

Father Feodor, looking greatly relieved, congratulated us and made his excuses to leave. To my surprise, the wedding then became something of a genteel social exchange, with people chatting in twos and threes, sipping glasses of champagne and nibbling blinis and caviar.

More than ever, I wanted to be alone with my wife – just calling her that gave me a thrill of happiness – but that was not allowed to happen. Serge and Madame Lili split us up, and the old 'Cossack', after pumping my hand in another rather forced display of bonhomie, took me to one side and asked what was troubling me. I told him simply that I'd thought that Russian weddings were supposed to be lively affairs, with much drinking and dancing and gipsy music.

'But of course, Nico!' he cried, slapping me on the shoulder so hard that I staggered backwards. 'Of course. Tonight you will have your dancing and you will never forget it!'

So it seemed that this was not the reception but merely the finale of the marriage service. The real festivities would begin later that evening, and I would see what a Russian wedding was really like!

That was all well and good, but it meant that Natalie and I would now be parted until the celebrations began, when all I wanted was for us to be together. Nothing could be done to change things, however, so I tried to accept the situation philosophically.

I should have been looking forward to it – there hadn't been many parties in this House! But something – I don't know what – was niggling at the back of my mind, a feeling of uneasiness that I could not shake off.

## CHAPTER 11

# Danse Macabre

*'Thy dead men shall live;*
*Together with my dead body shall they arise.*
*Awake and sing, ye that dwell in dust.'*

ISAIAH 26:19

Towards early evening, Serge came to find me in my room. He had changed into an odd-looking costume with dark breeches and a long black cloak; this was my first clue that the 'ball' was to be a masque with elaborate costumes, though mine, which he carried over his arm, was simple enough: black breeches, knee-length boots, a white Russian shirt, buttoned at the side, and a plain black eye-mask.

In his huge right hand, Serge carried a half-bottle of champagne and a glass. Still wary of what might have been put into my drinks in the past, I'd intended to forgo drinking this evening, but relented on this occasion since he opened the bottle in front of me and poured a glass immediately, though refusing it himself on the excuse that he had been drinking vodka.

The champagne cheered me up and, two glasses later, I was suitably kitted up in my costume and pulling on the tall leather riding boots, hoping that I would not be required to execute any fancy dancing steps in them. The white shirt was a tight fit, and we decided that it could be left undone at the neck. By the time I had finished the third glass, I felt much more cheerful and began to look forward to the rest of the evening. I had never been to a masked ball before, and the ones I had seen on films seemed a bit sinister, but I was prepared to have an open mind.

The next surprise was the venue. Serge explained that, instead of the huge dining room where the séance had taken place, a room had been prepared 'in the attic'. By this, he meant above the third floor where most of the staff lived in a series of beamed mansard rooms, cramped and basic. There was, he said, a large 'loft' in the roof space, long disused, but now brought back into service as a ballroom of sorts, and this was, according to him, very 'atmospheric'.

As we left my rooms, Anya appeared, looking quite lovely in an exotic flowing costume that I thought made her look like Queen Guinevere in pictures of King Arthur's Court. She said that she had been sent to explain what was expected of me.

I was really pleased to see her. We had once been close, in a brother-and-sister way, and I felt guilty that I had stupidly upset her at our last meeting in the garden when, thanks to my appalling drunken behaviour, we had parted in bad grace. Now it seemed she had forgiven me, and her presence beside me when we mounted the stairs was comforting and reassuring.

Leaving the second floor by the servants' stairs, we climbed to the third floor and entered a long, low corridor with small rooms either side where I knew the staff slept. At the far end of this narrow passageway, a tight spiral stairway of rough-hewn timber led up towards the attic. It was here that I had my first hint that all was not well. My legs seemed to give way and I grabbed the curving banister rail for support. Serge was behind me and pushed me forward and somehow I managed to step on to the small landing at the top. There, Anya caught up with us and fussed around me, mumbling about how I should learn to drink champagne more slowly…

It was hot up there, close to the roof timbers, and airless, with a very musty smell, but I reasoned that I would be all right once we were in a larger space. Anya opened a small, low door and we emerged into a long, low mansard-windowed hall, so brightly lit that I blinked behind my mask; it was a marked contrast to the soft glow of oil lamps in the rest of the House.

All the household staff were there and, as I grew used to the light, I could see the brilliant costumes and the stunning coloured drapes that hid the walls. I guessed that on this occasion the ban on electric lights had been lifted.

Truly dazzled by the light and colours of this reception, I tried to take in who was there. The costumes and weird bird-like masks reminded me of those I had once seen at a carnival in Venice. Masks were on sale all over that city, colourful, exquisite and artistic yet at the same time ugly, sinister and weird, as were these, and some of those wearing them!

In some cases, I recognised people by their figure and build and easily identified Agnès the maid and Amélie the cook. Voikin and Chermakov were also easy to spot, but I really had eyes only for Natalie, my wife; her lovely white close-fitting dress and long blonde hair marked her out as special, and the beaked eye mask with its glittering sequins could not disguise her.

Lifting her mask, she kissed me in a way that took my breath away, holding me to her with one hand on the lapel of my shirt and the other gripping the hair on the back of my head. At that moment, I could have forgone all the celebrations, the masked ball, the staff of the House, everything, just to be alone with my wife.

But, of course, it was not yet to be. I consoled myself with the thought that it could not now be long.

Somewhere at the back of the room, a wind-up gramophone with a huge horn speaker struck up a waltz, and I did not need Serge's urging to realise that I was expected to open the celebrations by dancing with my wife.

Natalya seemed so fragile in her long dress that, when I put my arm around her waist, I thought she might break. At first, I stepped out with a confidence that surprised me – dancing had never been one of my skills, but the waltz seemed easy enough and Natalie was as light as a feather. Around and around we went, my confidence growing in leaps and bounds.

I had never dreamed that I could be so happy. The House had dragged me down to the depths of despair, only to elevate me to a happiness I never knew existed. It seemed symbolic somehow that we were now at the very top of the House, as if having surmounted all its difficulties.

It must have been about halfway through the dance that I felt the effects of the champagne again – if, indeed, it was the champagne. My knees buckled without any warning, and had it not been for Natalie's quick supporting action I would have gone down. Recovering the beat, we carried on, only for me to trip and this time nearly drag Natalie down with me. Somehow she continued to hold me up, and we shuffled around in a parody of a dance until mercifully the music ceased.

Now I was sure that something was wrong. Two or three glasses of champagne could never have done that to me. In some way, I had been drugged again; but why? What could anyone gain by doing that to me at my own wedding?

The waltz ended, and drinks were again handed round, while someone wound up the gramophone. I refused everything and Natalie stood beside me, stoically holding my arm and secretly supporting me.

It was stiflingly hot there under the eaves and the lights seemed unnaturally bright, and so intense as to be oppressive. The dancing began again and this time everyone joined in, masks in place and looking really weird to my befuddled mind. Gallantly Natalie held on to me, and we stood together in silence as everyone danced around us. I was so ashamed to be like that and wanted desperately to dispel the notion that I was too drunk to dance with my wife on our wedding night. Somehow I *had* to overcome whatever had been secretly given to me.

I stood up straight, took a deep breath, and concentrated on shaking off the malaise that had almost overcome me.

All might have been well except for the arrival of someone who, in spite of her elaborate costume and mask, I knew well. Madame Lili, her lovely face hidden behind the sinister mask of a raven and dressed head to foot in black, cut in on us, while Chermakov drew Natalie away.

Madame Lili's overwhelming perfume would have given her away whatever costume she wore, and now she held on to me with a strength that surprised me.

'My dear, dear Nicolai Feodorovitch,' she whispered in my ear. 'How I have looked forward to dancing with you!'

She stepped off into the other dancers, dragging me with her. One of her hands held mine and the other she slipped inside my shirt and around my waist. Her gloves were damp against my skin and she gripped me so hard that it was painful. I tried, half-heartedly, to pull away, but it did no good. To my acute embarrassment, I found that the closeness of her body had invoked a physical response in me that no bridegroom should feel for another woman – especially on his wedding night. Pressed against me as she was, she could not fail to notice it, and, when she did, she lifted her mask and smiled at me in such a way that I could feel the colour flush in my face.

The music stopped. The gramophone was re-cranked. I suppose I should have tried to get away from Madame Lili then but I didn't. I just stood there, by her side, obediently. She, and the House, had broken me. Any self-assertion I might once have possessed had been left at the door, six weeks before.

The next dance was faster, much faster, and Madame Lili dragged me around and around, whirling through the hot, stuffy loft until the coloured drapes, the dresses and costumes became a kaleidoscope of moving shapes. Gripped so tightly by her gloved arms, I could not escape, nor could I feel my feet nor focus on other people or objects. It seemed to me that the lights were growing dim and, though pleased at first for a respite from the glare, I became daunted at the growing darkness. The overlit room shrank to a tiny dot and then went out completely as the floor rushed up to meet me.

The floor was hard and the bare planks smelled of dust and decay. An intense blackness enveloped me and the heavy silence was broken only by a sh…sh…sh…sound that I eventually recognised as the noise of the gramophone needle turning in its end-groove.

My disorientation was complete. Where was I? Where were the wedding guests? And where was my wife, Natalie?

Lifting my face from the floor, I managed to sit up and strained my eyes to look around. The blackness stared back with just a slight shimmer here and there, edged with a deeper black. Instinctively, I felt there were others in the room; somewhere, beyond the blackness, there was a presence. Something was about to happen and, whatever it might be, I sensed that I was not going to like it. The feeling of expectancy was palpable.

Softly, the tone of the unseen gramophone changed to a low, almost imperceptible note, followed immediately by another the same and then another, and I realised it sounded like a clock striking. When it reached twelve, it ceased, only to be followed by a slow, weird tune, each note a little clearer than the first, until they formed a slow, soft, eerie refrain. Very slowly, the music continued, gathering in momentum and strength – a weird, haunting melody that, even confused as I was, I recognised as one of the few pieces of classical music I was familiar with: St-Saëns' 'Danse macabre'.

On the floor, in pitch darkness, bewildered and afraid, I felt the music more intensely than anything I had ever heard before, the strange, haunting melody sending shivers up my spine.

My instinct was to stand up, but my reason told me to stay on the floor. If I managed to stand, what could I do and where could I go in such complete darkness? My heart pounded in my chest and my eyes ached from trying to peer into the blackness that surrounded me.

The music slowly began to gather momentum and increase in volume, and I found that I was shaking with fear of the unknown.

Again, I stared into the blackness all about me and, this time, I felt as though I could detect movement – a swirling of the darkness, gradually becoming dark grey and then grey: it was lifting, almost imperceptibly changing into a gloomy, misty dawn.

I watched, fascinated, as the swirling movements became gradually clearer and slowly came into focus. I gave a sudden start and my heart began to pound as I watched the grey shapes morph into figures, figures of human bones – skeletons dancing slowly all around me.

The safety valve in my brain must have cut off the adrenaline and replaced it with a burst of logic – these were the guests, my wedding guests, dressed in black with white bones painted…to scare me…of course! But, even as I thought it, doubt broke in. Was it even possible that the 'motley crew' of house guests, men and women, all shapes and sizes, in different elaborate costumes, could have changed into this? Again, the cold fingers of disbelief curled around my spine. Who would inflict this upon me on my wedding night?

Until that time I had only half-believed in the concept of evil, but now my head ached from trying to understand. 'Madness' was my ultimate conclusion.

The music was reaching its crescendo, the dead swirling around me, drawing the circle closer and closer…

Then, abruptly, it stopped. Darkness returned, only to be followed within seconds by a single white floodlight, and there, caught in its beam, my bride, resplendent in her white bridal gown, blonde hair hanging down her slender back and face hidden behind her veil… Natalya…

Fighting off my giddiness and the malaise that gripped me still, I crawled towards her, perspiring from the effort and concentrating on every move.

'Natalie!'

I heard my voice, a trembling, croaking, disembodied sound.

'Natalie!'

Staggering to my feet, I reached out to her, the light dazzling. I seized her arm and lifted up her veil with the other hand.

And there, in place of that beautiful pale and delicate face, grey-blue eyes and classic features, was a skull. Black, empty eye-sockets and fleshless, snarling mouth, the teeth clenched in a terrifying rictus.

I jumped back and her arm, its skeletal hand in mine, came with me. The skeleton tilted towards me, its fleshless face pressed close to mine, and then seemed to explode into fragments of sharp bone and clouds of filthy, choking dust.

I could hear myself shrieking and tried frantically to get away but, as I stepped back, I came up against something solid, something living, and with it the cloying, oppressive perfume of Madame Lili. I remember looking down to see the remains of my wife fall in a broken heap and explosion of dust on the floor. As I tried to back away, I felt the strong arms of Serge encircle me from behind. Another gust of perfume, a sting in my arm and then the sensation of falling…falling, head-first, into a dark, deep well.

'…and lo, the bones were very dry. And the Lord said to me: "Son of Man, can these bones live?" And I answered: "Oh Lord God, Thou Knowest".'

EZEKIEL 37:2–3

## CHAPTER 12

# The Betrayal

*'Just because you don't believe in it, it doesn't mean you're safe.'*

ANYA

I don't know what woke me. Perhaps it was the unwonted coming and going past my door or the distant mumble of voices in a house usually so quiet and still.

Giddiness hit me as soon as I sat up, and I had to wait a few moments before I could even attempt to stand.

Horrific memories of the night burst into my mind; I had no defences. To try to blot them out, I concentrated on standing up. My legs shook, feeling as though at any moment they would let me down and send me crashing to the floor.

I must have slept clothed. There were small splashes of blood on my shirt, and my hands were cut and sore. The metal of the bed frame supported me, and I clung to it until my knuckles showed white.

Far, far away in the House, I could hear voices, and footsteps going to and fro. There were other noises too, of things – furniture – being moved, and bumps and squeaks, and always the constant murmur of voices.

A step away from my trusty support left me swaying alarmingly, but I stayed upright and tentatively moved towards the door. Triumphantly, I grasped the handle and pulled, only to discover that it was locked and there was no longer a key in the keyhole. A lurch to the right propelled me into my tiny sitting room, and from there I tottered into the schoolroom. Here, the door was also locked and no key to be found. Why was I locked in? What was happening that necessitated my being kept prisoner in my own rooms?

Feeling slightly stronger, I made it across to the big front window. Looking down on to the driveway below, I could see the roofs of two large removal vans and, though I could not see anyone, I could hear voices coming from near the front door. The windows would not open and I sank on to the nearest chair with the realisation that I had been deliberately isolated from whatever momentous events were taking place.

Anger welled up inside me, a feeling of abuse and betrayal that was long overdue. This House, these people, were deliberately humiliating me; they had been all along, and I had known it but, for so many reasons, allowed it to happen. A long, slow, carefully plotted betrayal.

With a sudden clarity, I understood what I must long have known and yet subconsciously suppressed. I was a rat in an experiment, the willing victim of some sort of vicious parlour game, taken to extreme lengths and, presumably, satisfying someone's sadistic, sick idea of pleasure. Vague notions of vengeance and retribution swept around my muddled brain, but how, and against whom? One thought overrode everything: where was Natalie? What had they done to her? Surely she could never be part of this evil game?

My one need now was to get out of these locked rooms and confront my tormentors, rescue Natalie and get away from this

House. And then I remembered the 'secret' stairway that led down to the mezzanine of the library.

I jumped up and promptly hit the floor again. Carefully this time, I got to my feet and slowly moved towards the schoolroom cupboard, tottering like a child learning to walk. Once inside the cupboard, I pushed the wall and gasped with relief when it swung open on to the narrow stair. This was much easier to deal with than walking, as there were rails either side to hold on to and little room to fall.

At the mezzanine balcony, I moved slowly along to the top of the small spiral stairway leading to the ground floor. From there, I could look down into the library, as I had done so many weeks before, spying on Madame Lili.

My eyes were still not focusing properly, but I could see through the open library doors into the great hall, where tremendous comings and goings were taking place. The front doors of the House were both open and I could see the side of a large van parked on the gravel drive. A man I did not recognise was shutting the back doors and talking to another man who looked a lot like Serge except that he was dressed in jeans and a T-shirt. There were voices on the grand staircase, and two women came into view as they descended into the hall. One was a tall, slender blonde, and the other, only slightly shorter, had short brown hair.

I concentrated my eyes on them and steadily they both came into focus. The brunette was Madame Lili and the blonde Natalya! Both wore jeans and T-shirts.

I must have let out some sort of groan, or at least an expression of surprise, because both looked up as if they had heard something. Fortunately, they didn't look in my direction, and I was able to get on to the spiral stair. Gripping the rails as tightly as I could in my weakened state, I crept slowly downwards. Steadying myself on the last step, I lurched into the library, supporting myself against the billiard table, and swung towards the open doors leading to the hall. Anger and dismay drove me on as I made it to the doorway, and it was only then that the two women looked up.

They seemed so shocked to see me that, for a moment, they did not react.

I tried to call out to Natalie but managed only a hoarse croak. The look on their faces turned from surprise to dismay. I had almost reached them now and summoned one final lurch that brought me close enough to touch them.

Then, suddenly, Serge appeared beside me and, before I could react, I felt a heavy blow to the right side of my head. It poleaxed me and, once again, I was flat out on the floor. Madame Lili said something in German and, out of focus, I saw Serge's feet retreat towards the front door. Now she was shouting to Natalie and I heard my wife's light footfall moving away.

I smelled rather than saw the ever-fragrant Madame Lili beside me. She pulled me over on to my front and then knelt with all her weight on the back of my right arm, high up near the shoulder, pinning me to the floor and sending stabs of pain up to my neck. She said nothing. After a few moments, I saw Natalie's feet approaching, level with my line of sight. I sensed her hand something to Madame Lili. Again they spoke in German, and Natalie, somewhat reluctantly it seemed, knelt on my left side, holding my arm to the floor as Madame Lili thrust a needle into my shoulder, swearing softly in German and making no attempt to be gentle.

Whatever she gave me, it seemed to take an age to go in, and I felt every drop of it. Nor did it render me immediately unconscious; after they both got off me, I was able to roll over on to my back. I knew, though, that I could not get up.

Slowly, very slowly, I started to feel my limbs grow weaker. There was no feeling of drowsiness or loss of consciousness, at least not at first, and although paralysed I was able to watch the events of the House drawing to a close. The men outside finished closing the van doors and called to the women to join them. Madame Lili loomed over me, a cold, dispassionate face, devoid of any sign of pity and bordering on disgust.

'Farewell, Nicolai Feodorovitch!' she mocked. 'You've had your five minutes of fame. As you say in English – "Every dog has his day"!' And she went out of view, laughing at her own joke.

I felt now that my betrayal was almost complete and lost all will to fight or resist.

Natalie appeared, kneeling beside me; she had been crying and her face was streaked with tears.

'Nico,' she sobbed. 'I know you will never be able to forgive me for what we've…I've, done to you. But you need to know that…' her voice cracked '…that I really did love you. It wasn't meant to be like this.'

Even if I had been able to reply, I had nothing left to say to her. Blackness was circling the edge of my vision and I watched her walk out of my view as through a telescope; the hole that was my vision became smaller and smaller and finally closed on blackness. Even then, I could still hear the sound of the vans driving away, crunching on the gravel of the narrow driveway.

Then all was silence, and the fear of Death.

I was frightened; more scared than words are able to express. I was paralysed and trapped in my body, unable even to call out, and it terrified me – a waking nightmare.

I must have been unconscious for a long time, because it was pitch black when I awoke but I sensed that I was still where I had fallen, in the great hall.

Although it was a warm summer's night, I felt cold; the chill of the tiled floor seeped up through my thin shirt into my back, but I was unable even to shiver.

The darkness of the hall was absolute. Had I been able to move enough to see behind me, there might have been a vestige of grey around the huge windows, but the blackness seemed to close in on me like an almost palpable fog.

Perhaps I was dead! Perhaps that is what Death is – trapped in a body no longer able to function, unable to move, unable to see through the blackness, yet with a mind that continues to function or, at least, continues to think and perceive. The thought appalled me.

I closed my eyes and then opened them again. Darkness has no boundary; it was drowning me.

I have always been afraid of the dark. Living in Paris, it didn't matter; the streets and shops were lit all night. Electric light is the death of ghosts. Out in the countryside in England where I was born, we were taught to be wary of the dark and respectful of places where instinctively we felt uncomfortable at night and where you couldn't take a horse, even in daytime.

Now, here in this House, I was very afraid; so afraid and so helpless that my only salvation lay in sleep. When I was unconscious, knowing and feeling nothing, I was safe. The danger was in my mind. Now I prayed for sleep, my only escape from an unbearable situation. There was no way to know whether my paralysis was permanent or even if the drug would kill me, but just a faint hope that I could escape into sleep and perhaps, if it was meant to be, wake up back in my old viable body.

But, to torment me further, sleep refused to come. Perhaps it was the chill in my bones or the fear in my mind. I remained stubbornly conscious.

Then, I heard it. I could not, at first, be sure. Then it came once more and I could no longer pretend that I was mistaken.

I was not alone. Way off in the depths of the House, something stirred.

I lay straining to identify those strange sounds – sounds that I sensed more than heard.

Now it came on, clearer and more regular: a slow, shuffling movement that I gradually realised was a faint, light footfall. Paralysis notwithstanding, I felt the hair bristle on my neck.

Slowly, but inexorably, it moved towards me up the long corridor from the back of the House. A pause, a faint sound that could have been a sigh, and then the footfall resumed, less hesitant than before, as if it now knew that I was there.

Instinctively, the 'fight or flight' mechanism kicked in, and adrenaline flooded through me, but my body had no response. I tried desperately to encourage the fear in the hope that I might faint, but remained alert with no escape.

The footfall was louder now and I guessed that whatever it was had left the carpeted corridor and was now moving along the tiled floor towards me.

Eventually it stopped. The feet wearing those shoes must have been level with my head but I saw nothing – nothing but the blackness that seemed to swirl around me.

Then suddenly everything changed as the movement close to me stirred the air and, on it, the unmistakable fragrance of Jasmin de Corse. The paralysis of my body focused my senses to such a degree that the perfume seemed almost overwhelming and with it came almost total relief – for this person next to me, still unseen in the darkness, was Tatiana Nicolaevna Romanova.

Even though she spoke in a whisper, her voice startled me.

'Oh, Nicolai, what have they done to you?'

The air moved again around my face and I sensed that she was closer, kneeling behind my head. A cool, soft hand touched my face with infinite tenderness, her fingers gently exploring the swelling that must have been on my cheek. With great care, she lifted my head and placed something soft beneath it. I could not, of course, answer her question, and wondered how she could see me in the darkness. The soft voice came again.

'How much evil there is in the world, Nico! I will pray for you now and, if you wish it, I will stay with you – always. How to explain to you, my Nicholas? Try to understand. There is Truth and there are Lies; there is fiction and there is fact; there is Life and there is Death; and then there are the spaces in between.'

I felt that I had just been told something of momentous importance, a revelation of some sort, but was unable to understand it. Now that I felt safe, my mind seemed to let go and started to drift away, as if leaving my body in Tatiana's safe keeping and seeking rest elsewhere. A great feeling of relief swept over me, and the soft warmth of her hand on my cheek was the last thing I can remember.

The sunshine streaming through the great windows of the hall warmed my cold, stiff body and, when it reached my face, woke me up. The hall was now a kaleidoscope of colours from the stained glass panels reflected from the black and white tiled floor.

I tried to sit up and failed, but realised at the same time that I could move my arms, and my legs too – after a clumsy, leaden fashion. I lay back and explored the movement of each muscle in turn and, when satisfied that they were no longer paralysed, I tried again to sit up. This time it worked, and from my new position I was able to look around me. I was quite alone, with no sign of Tatiana or, indeed, any other presence in the House.

My only thought now was to get out, and I concentrated all my efforts on standing up. Unable to do so from a sitting position, I rolled over on to my front, pushed up with my arms and drew my knees up under me. I stayed like that for a long time, waiting for the dizziness to clear. Then, with a great effort, stood up. I staggered a bit but, with my feet further apart than usual, I regained my balance. The first step was a lurch forward, then another, heading towards the front doors and stopping to fight the giddiness after each movement. My legs seemed to be following a plan of their own and only reluctantly obeyed my directions. With their eventual compliance, I reached the doors.

To my great relief, the door handle turned in my trembling hand and the doors swung inward, allowing a great shaft of sunlight to fall upon the chequered floor. With the sunshine came the soft warm breeze of a perfect summer's day. I stood there for a long time, breathing deeply and looking out across the drive and lawns towards the gates.

When I thought I felt strong enough, I lurched through the doorway and, thinking that I would fall, staggered quickly across the gravel towards the grass, and fell there. Though down on my knees, I fancied that I felt strong enough to continue. Closing my eyes, I waited for the giddiness to clear before rising and slowly moving off towards the huge green-painted portal that contained the smaller grille door reserved for pedestrians.

It seemed to take an age to cross the lawn, but every halting step was a step away from that House – a step towards freedom.

There was no one about. I sensed that the House was now deserted, but I expected to see people in the lane outside the railings. Again, to my relief, the small gate was not locked and I was out on to the drive leading to the main road.

I was warmer by then and beginning to feel very tired but I needed to go on, to reach the main boulevard. What I intended to do then had not yet come to me… I just knew a desperate need to find someone to help me get away from that place.

I heard the main road before I saw it, a glorious low roar of traffic, and when at last it came into view I blinked at the speeding cars, the sun flashing off their windscreens, gliding onwards as if in another world. A dark green public bench stood nearby and I collapsed on to it, unable to go further. I slumped back and the warm sunshine fell upon my face. I closed my eyes and listened to the hum of the traffic.

When I woke up in hospital, I couldn't remember anything at first and just lay back dozing and watching the nurses occasionally walk by. Later, as my memory returned, I started to feel very anxious. If, as it would seem, I had been found unconscious beside the road, the police would surely have been informed, and once they started to interview me they would find out that I had no papers and I would surely go to prison – either for that or for vagrancy. I began to consider ways to escape, except that my clothes had been taken away and I knew that I couldn't walk very far.

As much as I dared, I confided in the young doctor who attended me. It seemed that, since the student riots, the police were far too busy to concern themselves with vagrants and *toxicomanes* (druggies), and that was apparently what the doctor thought I was.

A counsellor came to see me and I made up some story about some friends tricking me into 'doing' some drugs and that I wasn't really an addict. I think I was saved by giving the address of the House as my fixed abode. Anyway, after a couple more days they released me into the care of the British Embassy, who, grudgingly, advanced me a small sum of money under the guarantee of reimbursement by funds from my family, which happily had been released during my stay in the House. After that, I was left in peace; except that 'peace' was far from describing my state of mind.

# Dénouement

# Dr Gröller's Conclusions

*'For now we see through a glass, darkly; but then face to face: now I know in part.'*

1 CORINTHIANS 13:12

Reading Nicholas's account had a profound effect on me. For the first time, I realised that I might be out of my depth in taking on his case so confidently. Frankly, I did not know how to begin to treat him.

The first step was to obtain a second opinion. My father had recently retired from his job as a *commissaire* in the Judicial Police and I valued his layman's opinion. His immediate reaction was that we were dealing with a crime – a conclusion not wholly unexpected, and a valid point of view. His contention was simply that Nicholas was the victim of a horrendous deception practised on him by the whole household over the period of his six-week stay in that House. He pointed out that hallucinogenic drugs had been detected in Nicholas's system when he was hospitalised, and that he had apparently been blackmailed into marrying Natalya.

The problem with that was the lack of evidence in the hospital report and the fact that Nicholas actually *wanted* to marry Natalya anyway.

Nicholas himself had arrived at similar conclusions and, as soon as he could afford it, had hired a firm of private detectives to make enquiries. My father immediately offered to open an investigation of his own, and Nicholas enthusiastically accepted.

It was, however, soon apparent that the perpetrators of this 'scam', if that was what it was, had covered their tracks extremely well. All transactions relating to the rental and running of the House were made either in cash or through an overseas bank account which was closed just before the House was vacated. The references for the tenants were false. Local tradesmen were likewise paid in cash. Attempts to trace individuals also came to nothing. No Dr Voikin was listed as licensed to practise medicine in France, nor was any Chermakov certified to practise law. The Russian Orthodox Church in Paris had never heard of a Father Feodor, and none of the servants could be traced.

Madame Lili, Natalya and the Grand Duchess were not known to the extensive Russian exile community in Paris, nor could they be traced historically.

In short, to his total exasperation, my father drew a complete blank. Nor did the private detectives fare any better, in spite of an exhaustive search for Anya both in France and Belgium (because Nicholas thought he had detected a Belgian accent in her French).

All this careful subterfuge only reinforced my father's contention that Nicholas was the victim of a very clever deception carried out by consummate professionals. But the motive completely escaped him. And, without proof that a crime had been committed, the magistrate would not open a dossier and pursue the enquiries further.

None of this helped me decide how to treat my patient. Fortunately, writing down his own account of the 'incident' did seem to help Nicholas to some extent, and he appeared a little less intense and obsessive. But he was far from well, and his mental state worried me. Finally, I consulted with more experienced colleagues. The unanimous conclusion was that Nicholas's condition would not improve until he could be confronted with the truth – the 'explanation' of what happened to him and why.

So we were back to square one. My father continued to plug away at his enquiries and I and Dr David did our best to care for Nicholas, but none of us with much success.

The publication of this book * was intended as a last attempt – a somewhat desperate appeal to those who might know some answers. With Nicholas's full consent and co-operation, I wrote it as an appeal for help, asking any readers who might know something to come forward to help solve this mystery.

This was a most unusual step for any psychiatrist to take, and some would see it as highly unorthodox. I justify it, however, by my professional opinion that only by removing the uncertainty and mystery surrounding Nicholas's 'unsettling experience' could we halt his slow decline into clinical depression.

*_refers to the original French edition_

# Breakthrough

*'The case is one where we have been compelled to reason backwards from effects to causes.'*

SIR ARTHUR CONAN DOYLE

The previous text was the conclusion of the original French edition, but it so happened that, before the English translation of this book could go to press, a sudden breakthrough changed the whole course of events.

My father called me in a state of great excitement, unusual for him, and almost shouted, 'It's all about the suits!'

Confused, I repeated, 'The suits?'

'All the clothes,' he said with exultation, and abruptly hung up.

We met a short time later in a local café, and I could see from the smug look on his face that he had something momentous to tell me.

'It was the suits, you see, the clothes they gave Nicholas at that house.'

He paused for effect and for me to ask, 'What about them?'

'They fitted him perfectly, didn't they? Even the shirt collars and the shoes!'

In his excitement he was almost shouting, and several customers looked up. I could only agree, wondering where he was going with this.

'Well, don't you see? They were for *him*, Nicholas, and him alone. *They were expecting him!*' he shouted, emphasising the words by banging the table with the flat of his hand, oblivious to the annoyed looks from the other coffee-drinkers.

I let the words sink in, but failed to see the significance.

'They were expecting him and only him,' my father said again, lowering his tone to normal levels. The other customers resumed their conversations. 'They knew *he* was coming and that nobody else would answer their advertisement. And how could that be?' he asked rhetorically. 'Because he was the only one who saw that job listed. I checked the papers for that whole week. There were no advertisements at all for that position. He was "the chosen one", so to speak.'

'But, Papa, Nicholas saw the ad. His friend Bruno showed it to him…' I protested.

But my father was already shaking his head. 'He saw a photocopy of what he took to be a newspaper advertisement, a quarter of a page, not the paper itself. Don't you see what this means, Marie-Claire? It means that we must find Bruno and ask him where he got the ad.'

And find him we did, coming out of a class at the Ecole Polytechnique.

We pounced on him, our intensity startling him, and took him with us to a café to question him. He was quick to explain that he had been given the photocopy of the advertisement by Nicholas's tutor, Professor S.– H.–, the one Nicholas didn't take to overmuch but who had been kind enough to let him stay at his flat for a few days, an ideal opportunity to ascertain the sizes of all his clothes. He would certainly have known of Nicholas's predicament, his isolation and his lack of family contacts in Paris.

Unfortunately, Professor Robert S.– H.– had disappeared from Paris a few months previously, having resigned his post shortly after Nicholas entered the House. Apparently his East European political leanings were a little too much for an establishment reeling from a student revolt.

My father was lost in thought, avidly studying Nicholas's account, which he'd had typed and carried with him. Poor Bruno seemed completely lost, left out of our blinding revelations, yet the cause, indirectly, of most of them. I felt so sorry for him. He appeared to believe that he was the initial author of all Nicholas's woes but he was just as much of an innocent dupe as Nico himself. What could I possibly say to enlighten him without hours of explanation? My father saved the day by paying for our drinks, heartily shaking hands with Bruno and thanking him profusely.

My father was like a bloodhound on the scent of a trail, and, though our quarry had gone to ground, the logic of his theory was gradually coming together. For my part, I was groping for my own leads; something about the Professor's name was ringing bells in the depth of my mind. Then suddenly it came to me: S.– H.– was the surname of Dr Ulrika S.– H.–, whose theories and experiments had caused outrage in psychiatric circles a few years previously in the mid-sixties, and who had disappeared into East Germany before she could be formally struck off. Nowadays, Dr Ulrika S.– H.– was East Germany's foremost authority on mind control. She spent the early part of the sixties experimenting with the use of new drugs at that time called, collectively, hallucinogens, the best known being LSD. These drugs were also being investigated by the CIA with a view to using them for mind control, previously known as 'brainwashing' when they were used by the Chinese during the war in Korea. Considered highly unethical by the psychiatric profession, S.– H.– fought back against the establishment with several well-researched papers expounding her theories before disappearing behind the Iron Curtain, presumably to the East German Stasi – their secret police – and other Soviet Bloc secret services.

Unfortunately, our further research into Dr Ulrika drew a blank, except for two things – which my father fastened upon triumphantly. She was young, dark-haired and very beautiful, and she apparently had a younger sister who, when last heard of, was studying acting in Vienna. Both sisters, though German, had been educated in Switzerland and were known to be bilingual in French. Here then, according to my father's theory, were 'Madame Lili' and 'Natalya'.

I had not seen my father so animated since before his retirement, and he hastened to fit more parts of his jigsaw together. Although his ideas were still only a proposition, the clincher for me was the mention of hallucinogenic drugs. Such chemicals are known to produce the sorts of symptoms or 'trips' that would fit many of the experiences described by Nicholas. I was certain that drugs had, on occasion, been administered to him orally, in his tea or wine, and we knew that, towards the end, he had been injected, but the real revelation came from something Nicholas had mentioned on several occasions: that Madame Lili always wore gloves and these often felt damp when she held him tightly either by his hands or wrists or, at least once, with her gloved hands inside his shirt and round his waist.

Now, hallucinogens are readily absorbed through the skin; by wearing waterproof surgical gloves under her long dress gloves, Madame Lili could easily moisten the material – probably silk – with the drug and administer it to Nicholas by touching his bare skin for just a few moments; the longer the contact, the greater the dose, but nonetheless difficult to control precisely, and therefore dangerous to the recipient.

The more I thought about it, the more certain I became. Nicholas could have been drugged at will and not been aware that it was happening.

Equally obvious to me was that some form of hypnosis had frequently been used on Nicholas, and I determined to find out what skills the good doctor had in that department.

Back at my practice rooms, I decided not to contact Nicholas until our theory had been further tested. My next step was to research Dr Ulrika, and particularly to try to find a photograph of her.

In this, I was unsuccessful as she proved to be very camera-shy. In fact, there was very little information on public record concerning her except for an old CV, listing where she had been educated and what qualifications she held. Even this information had not been updated for several years. It seemed that she had been completely ostracised by the medical profession.

My father hoped for better results, and yet he too was frustrated; it was true that both the DST and SDECE – the French internal and external security services – apparently held files on her, but these could not be made available to the police, and certainly not to a retired *commissaire*. By calling in all sorts of favours, however, he was able to glean at least some negative information. Dr S.– H.– was not of any 'active' interest and her current whereabouts were unknown, believed to be in the Soviet Bloc.

My father even thought about calling in a retired police artist to draw portraits from Nicholas's descriptions but, with no photographs to compare them with and no witnesses to show them to, it seemed a pointless exercise. He then widened his searches to include the others at the House. Enquiries were made concerning both Anya and Serge. My father and his friends were most thorough, even checking Parisian theatrical costumiers to see if anyone answering Serge's description had hired a Cossack uniform.

Without specifically telling Nicholas why, we decided we would, after all, get him together with a retired police artist to produce portraits of Serge and Anya, and then we showed them around in the Russian community in the vicinity of the Alexander Nevsky Cathedral, where expats gather to go to services, drink tea and browse the Russian language bookshop. None of it did any good. Nobody knew them, knew of them or had even seen anyone like them.

My father's retirement took on a new lease of life; he felt he was useful again and, as he told my long-suffering mother, he felt this case was more baffling than anything he'd done before. He had been a senior officer for so long that I don't think my father could even remember the last time he had done any of the 'routine legwork' that he set so much store by, and he loved every minute of it, even though his 'robust' and 'direct methods' were, even then, barely acceptable to modern policing.

While all this was going on, I tried, between caring for my other patients, to assemble all the papers I could find concerning Dr S.– H.–'s published research. There wasn't much, and nothing specifically relating to Nicholas's ordeal. The general tenor, though, was towards influencing the subconscious mind, the parts that only intrude on consciousness when we are asleep or are somehow induced to override the usual responses of the perceptive half of the brain. To this end, she relied at first on previous experiments using drugs such as sodium pentothal, and then, following the lead of the CIA, hallucinogens. Hypnotism, for all its reputation in the popular imagination, played a very small part. Mesmerism, and then hypnotism, are surrounded by myths. At least one in five people cannot be hypnotised, and even those susceptible and who can be put into a deep, trance-like state cannot be persuaded to perform any act that they would refuse to do when awake. Programming people to commit crimes or assassinations at a given command remains, at least at the time of writing this, a fiction.

That is not to say that hypnosis does not exist as a useful weapon for the psychiatrist or hypnotherapist, and there is some evidence that Madame Lili practised it on Nicholas, primarily to relax him and make his mind more receptive to suggestion when the drugs began to take effect, and perhaps allow her to control the 'trip' to some extent. Several times in his account, Nicholas states that, while holding his bare arms with her damp gloves, Madame Lili spoke to him softly but firmly: 'Look at me, Nicholas. Listen to me, Nicholas. Listen to my voice…' These are classic prompts used in hypnosis ever since Anton Mesmer began practising it on his subjects. It says something for Madame Lili's skill that she was able to have such a marked effect on Nicholas, because he is one of the twenty per cent of people who do not normally respond to hypnotism. I know this because I tried to treat him with hypnotherapy myself, with little useful result.

Meanwhile, we kept Nicholas in the dark until some concrete evidence turned up.

Such evidence was slow in coming. There were, of course, bits and pieces dribbling in. For example, I managed to obtain Nicholas's medical records from his short stay in hospital. They mentioned only what we already knew: 'A contusion was present on the right malar bone with resultant oedema and discoloration.' In other words, a swollen, bruised cheekbone.

This matched Nicholas's description of the blow that had felled him before he was finally injected.

More disappointing was the toxicology report, which listed only that 'a substance known to be hallucinogenic was found in high quantities in the blood', and was specific neither in the name of the drug nor in the actual amount. It seems that, having found traces of drugs in Nicholas's blood, the hospital doctors had believed that the origin of his symptoms had been ascertained, and the police had considered this an acceptable explanation for his being found unconscious in a public place. In short, they believed that they were dealing with a 'junkie', and that was the end of any credibility his story might once have had. No one thought to submit him to a psychiatric evaluation.

Eventually, my father succeeded in getting permission to visit the House itself, which was undergoing redecoration prior to being re-let. Again I judged it better not to tell Nicholas of our intended visit, and spent an afternoon with my father examining the House and grounds.

It was very much as Nicholas had described it, and his detail had been so accurate that I actually felt I recognised certain parts, particularly the great entrance hall with its dual staircases.

We visited on a bright sunny day, which showed the huge stained glass windows at their best, and the House appeared cheery and bright. But the sky clouded over after a while and then things took on quite a different aspect. The windowless corridors became gloomy and oppressive, and I could well imagine how eerie they must have seemed at night, lit only by a handful of oil lamps.

My father was particularly interested to see if he could find evidence of what he called 'electronic trickery' or hidden microphones, but found nothing except some wires leading to Nicholas's bedroom and study.

Although the use of electricity was formally not allowed in the main parts of the House, there was some evidence of its use in the staff bedrooms under the roof: a television aerial connection lead hung from one wall, and adaptor plugs were found, of the sort used for hairdryers. Here and there, items of discarded make-up were in evidence, but little else.

I was particularly interested in the room used by 'Dr Voikin' as his surgery, but there the clean-up had been very thorough and no drugs or syringes were found.

When I rejoined my father in the library, he was debating whether it was worthwhile collecting any fingerprints from various parts of the House in the vain hope that any of the previous occupants might be on file at the Criminal Records Office. He decided against such an arduous and probably unproductive approach. He did, however, spend a considerable time walking the grounds or, more specifically, the boundaries, to see if there were any places where an outsider could gain access. Satisfied that the garden was secure, he joined me for a last look at the House from a distance, to see if there was any chance of a hidden room concealed in the roofline or any access points to the cellars.

At a nearby café, we sat and looked at each other, unable to draw any solid conclusions from our visit. I was glad that we had taken the trouble, though, because it enabled me to form some small idea of the closed and isolated atmosphere of the House and how uncannily remote it felt, even though it was just a couple of miles from the centre of Paris.

We drank our coffee in silence, my thoughts concentrated on how I could best 'sell' our theory to Nicholas, because, in spite of some compelling evidence, theory it still was.

On our return to Rueil-Malmaison, I called Nicholas, invited him to dinner at my parents' house and then drew up a set of notes, anticipating his questions.

After dinner, we – my father and I – took Nicholas into the study and, over drinks, told him that we had a theory. Nicholas was not surprised; he had suspected that I had news for him and, in spite of his stolid and relaxed appearance, I could see that he was seething with expectation.

Slowly and methodically, my father put our case to him. He readily agreed to my father's request not to interrupt until we had fully expounded our version of events, concentrating on the two main causes of Nicholas's anxiety: what exactly had taken place at the House, and why had it happened to him? Answer those two questions successfully, we reasoned, and the rest would more or less fall into place.

I observed Nicholas as my father set things out point by point. I could see that he had confidence in my father and that he appreciated it when he stopped and went back over areas that were based more on conjecture than fact. Both men were concentrating hard, my father to explain and Nicholas to understand. I sat, observed, and topped up their drinks. I knew better than to think that Nicholas would give much away, yet I felt somehow that he wasn't in disagreement. Naturally, he identified himself as the victim, and so it was essential for his mental wellbeing that we should be able to answer the 'why me?' question.

I could see that my theory of how the hallucinatory drugs were administered through the skin made perfect sense to him, and my ideas concerning Madame Lili's hypnotic and suggestive methods, and the way they could precondition him to see or experience certain things, satisfied his need to understand.

As my father's explanation drew to its conclusion, I was careful to add that, while we believed our deductions to be true, they were not the whole truth, but rather a framework to add future findings on and to allow us to analyse any such new information.

Finally, my father moved to what did *not* happen or, in other words, the parts of the plot that seemed to have gone wrong. He suggested to Nicholas that he was not supposed to have witnessed the departure of the house staff; that whatever sedative he had been given after that awful '*danse macabre*' of the skeletons had not been given in sufficient quantity to keep him unconscious while everyone left the premises; that Serge had struck him in a fit of panic rather than malice; that, while Madame Lili was clearly cold and dispassionate, the same might not have been true for her sister, Natalya. My father ventured that Natalie might well have fallen in love with Nicholas and thereby jeopardised the whole experiment.

As far as the pregnancy was concerned, he considered it pure fantasy invented only to heighten Nicholas's growing concern. It would have been very hard to tell that Natalie was pregnant after only three weeks. My father concluded with a passionate description of this 'monstrous deception' practised on a young man who was a hapless victim of very wicked people in pursuit of a despicable political aim.

After his heartfelt finale, my father sat back and took a sip of his brandy. The room fell oppressively silent. Nicholas, holding his own glass cupped in his hands, stared at the floor with unseeing eyes while no doubt his brain frantically computed all this new knowledge.

After what seemed an age, he looked up and asked the one question I was dreading.

'And what about Tatiana?'

Tatiana, I knew very well, was the weakest point in our theory. I could not explain her in any way that I felt would satisfy Nicholas.

At first, I had considered her as part of the whole deception – another occupant of the House whose role it was to confuse Nicholas and to bring a certain supernatural element to the plot and, perhaps, induce him to think he was losing his sanity. Equally she could, I thought, be an illusion planted in his mind by Madame Lili in the same way that she caused Nicholas to 'see' 'the monochromes', as he called them. But, even as I formulated that idea, I was forced to dismiss it. Tatiana was too real to Nicholas for me to ever convince him that she was an illusion. In a House full of deception and treachery, where nothing was as it seemed, she was the one person he felt he could rely on and indeed the only person who had stood by him during that dreadful night when he lay paralysed on the floor.

It seemed then increasingly clear that Tatiana was not part of the deception. Her rare appearance when others were present had caused chaos, with both Serge and Anya searching the House and grounds and Madame Lili constantly interrogating Nicholas. My father had found no way for someone to enter the grounds from outside, so who was she really? Where did she come from and where did she go?

The best I could do was to tell Nicholas that our enquiries were far from complete and that I was confident that Tatiana's presence in the House would eventually be explained.

It never was.*

*But see Epilogue.

# Epilogue

*'It is far harder to kill a phantom than reality.'*

VIRGINIA WOOLF

During the years since Nicholas wrote his harrowing account of what took place inside the House in those months of 1968, information about it has dropped to a bare trickle and nothing has come to light of an importance likely to resolve the mystery completely.

My father continued to study the various problems until his death in 1996, sadly with no major breakthrough. I believe he considered his inability to solve this case as the one great failure of his police career.

Private detectives employed by Nicholas abroad have contributed snippets of information here and there, basically confirming some of our conjectures about the identity of Madame Lili and her whereabouts in East Germany; but when the Wall came down in 1989 she was long gone and has not, to my knowledge, surfaced since, nor have any scientific papers concerning her methods and findings appeared in any international scientific journals for many years.

There was some excitement in 1991 when the detectives announced that they thought they had located Ulrika S.– H.–'s sister, 'Natalya' according to our hypothesis. A blurry snapshot was obtained showing a rather dowdy-looking woman leading two children down a street in one of the poorer districts of Vienna. Nicholas studied it for some time before coming to the conclusion that he could not be sure she was anyone he knew.

With the passing years, the trail has gone cold, and with it our chances of a definitive solution.

A theory must always be provisional. It may be possible for most results to agree with a hypothesis, but it takes only one contradiction to destroy it. It should, if a tenable theory, make predictions that may be tested in the fullness of time and, while there are many loose ends still, I am confident that overall what we have postulated is reasonably close to an explanation that Nicholas can accept.

The underlying dichotomy in Nicholas's character is that he is at once a romantic and a pragmatist. He finds it difficult to accept anything that cannot be proven to his satisfaction, and yet he faces a situation which can never be decisively resolved. He is most anxious that his sanity should not be called into question. Understandably, he is also very sensitive about any aspect of his experience in the House that might tend to suggest a supernatural origin, yet is frustrated that he often cannot find a logical explanation.

That said, there was a very marked improvement in both his mental and physical health after he had had time to digest our theory, and I believe that this demonstrates that he was, to a certain extent, convinced by it.

I say 'to a certain extent' because our explanation had the unfortunate effect of changing the question; it ceased to be 'Why me?' or even 'What was the meaning of it all?' and became less subjective. The question then for Nicholas became: 'Who or what was Tatiana?' Was she a figment of his imagination, planted there by Madame Lili, or was she a total interloper – an outsider who was unconnected with the scheme, an anomaly without explanation? There is also a third question that Nicholas avoids at all costs: was she a ghost, a spirit, a supernatural entity? To admit such a possibility, Nicholas instinctively feels, is the path to madness.

At the same time, while he was eventually prepared to accept the dissembling and betrayal of all the other denizens of the House, he could not bring himself to believe it of Tatiana. In his eyes she could never be like them; she was genuine, she was real, she did not deceive him, lie to him, ill-treat him or abuse him. She was his only true friend, who stayed with him to the bitter end. All these qualities, together with her artlessness and natural youthful beauty, were enough to make him fall in love with her – in retrospect. She was the only source of genuine affection in his life, excepting of course myself and my family, the only retrievable decent person in the whole of his 'unsettling experience', and he wasn't about to let go of her.

This became evident to me very soon after we had presented him with our theory. My father, always the practical policeman, thought that, once we had presented Nicholas with a compelling explanation, he would be released from his psychological burden and move on. To an extent, that is what happened, but my months of being with him, talking to him and treating him, gave me a deeper insight, and, though he tried to conceal it, I knew that any theory, no matter how plausible, that did not include and explain Tatiana was not going to be sufficient for his total recovery.

In the months and years that followed, I tried to formulate a theory that unified all the phenomena of the House. Slowly, very slowly, it seemed finally to be coming together.

Nevertheless, I had been retired for nearly a year when, after much hesitation, I felt able to call Nicholas and ask him to meet me.

We lunched in Rueil-Malmaison, outside at the small café opposite the church containing the tomb of the Empress Joséphine, her son Eugène and her daughter Hortense. Nicholas looked smart and well-groomed as usual, his boyish good looks now tempered by lines on his face and a definite greying of his hair around the temples. He appeared relaxed and carefree, smiling and joking, in an act, I was sure, put on for my benefit. We were no longer doctor and patient, but old friends at ease with each other.

We ate well and I kept our conversation on a casual basis. It was evident though that Nicholas was anticipating a more serious reason for my wanting to see him, and I thought it sensible to come to the point as soon as possible.

The meal finished and the wine bottle empty, we left the Beauharnais café and crossed the square towards Rue Jean le Coz and strolled up the narrow street in the direction of the Parc de Beaupréau. This park is one of my favourite places locally. Joséphine purchased the land to extend the grounds of the Château de Malmaison, where she and Napoléon lived together, and her garden there began at the far end of the park.

We chose a bench seat looking out across the small lake, quite private and warm in the sunlight. Nicholas stared down at the grass, waiting patiently.

'Well, Marie-Claire?' he said without looking up. 'What's on your mind?'

'What is on *my* mind, Nicholas, is what is on *your* mind. I'm your doctor, remember, or…at least I used to be, and I'm still trying to look after you.'

He turned towards me suddenly and said, straight-faced, 'You know, I should have married you; if you would have had me, of course.'

He must have seen the astonishment in my face, because he laughed to hide his embarrassment and tried to pass it off as a joke. In all the time I had known this man, he had never said or done anything that suggested the remotest hint of attraction, and the thought that he might have felt or might still feel any physical attraction for me had never crossed my mind. I must have blushed, and a look of panic came into his eyes.

'I'm so sorry, Marie-Claire, I didn't mean to embarrass you; I just wanted you to know how much I've appreciated what you and your family have done for me over all these years… I would be dead if it weren't for you.'

'Thank you, Nico, but…look, never mind all that. I want to tell you something I think is very important…'

I was trying to relieve his embarrassment. He nodded and resumed gazing out across the lake, the water rippling from the warm late afternoon breeze which had suddenly sprung up. I took a deep breath.

'Now, I have always thought that the one thing lacking in our enquiries into the "events" at the House was an explanation of the phenomenon known as Tatiana…'

'I don't know that "phenomenon" is quite how I would describe her,' he said, defensively.

'No, well, OK, Nico, I was speaking as a psychologist for a moment. Let us say "person" or "character" if it pleases you better…'

He nodded for me to continue.

'Now, what I've done is to go over your account, concentrating on the appearances of Tatiana, with reference to both your experiences and those of the others in the House who claimed to have seen her. OK?'

Again, he nodded. I took a deep breath, still uncertain that I was doing the right thing.

'This is what I've found. Every time Tatiana appeared to you, you were, by your own account, feeling unwell. We have already established that you were most often "unwell" due to the effects of the hallucinatory drugs that were being introduced into your nervous system in a variety of ways.'

Nicholas said nothing, but his frown demonstrated that I was not yet getting my argument across.

'Look, Nico, let's consider each sighting separately. The first was in the rose arbour the morning following your first meeting with Madame Lili. It was the first time Madame Lili had touched you with the famous "damp" gloves, the ones we are convinced were used to put the LSD or other hallucinogens into your system by absorption through the skin. You said you awoke with a headache, as if you had a hangover. You didn't eat much at breakfast, and you said that your meeting with Madame Lili had left you dizzy and light-headed. As you sat in the garden, you thought you saw some people who corresponded to the black and white photographs you had seen in your first glimpse of books about the Tsar and his family.

'Now, we know that the monochrome images you saw during your stay in the House were almost certainly hallucinations. Only one of the group in the garden was in colour, a young girl who waved at you. At the time, you believed them all to be from a neighbouring property.

'The next occasion was on the day following Natalya's attack on you as you slept. Dr Voikin gave Anya two small white tablets for you to take. Next day, you felt unwell and very tired. You had three cups of coffee at the table outside the kitchen, went into the garden, and fell asleep in the rose arbour, waking to find a girl there who introduced herself as Tatiana. After a fairly long and rather odd conversation, she seemed to disappear when Anya came looking for you.

'Next, she appeared at the séance. Afterwards, you drank a lot of vodka with Serge and this caused you to go to bed quite early. You soon slipped into what you describe as an uneasy, troubled sleep. You awoke when you thought that someone had slipped into your bed. You didn't actually see who it was, in the darkness, but afterwards you believed that person to have been Tatiana. You made love, after which she disappeared.

'Next, you saw her again in the garden after you had been threatened by Voikin and Chermakov with going to prison if you didn't marry Natalie and you had drunk almost a whole bottle of red wine. She appeared beside you, out of nowhere, and called you a "clumsy boy" for spilling wine on your shoes. After talking for some time, you closed your eyes for just a moment and then heard Madame Lili calling. When you looked up, Tatiana had disappeared.

'Then, finally, she came to you when you were drugged and paralysed on the floor of the great hall. It was pitch dark and, again, you did not actually see her.'

I paused to let all this sink in.

'So where is this heading, Marie-Claire?' he asked.

'I'm saying, Nicholas, that, though it may pain you greatly to admit it, Tatiana was, I am convinced now, a product of your subconscious, an illusion, just like the White Russian generals in the library, the Red Army soldier who "split" your skull after your horse died, the family in the garden, and the appalling skeleton bride you danced with at your wedding masked ball.'

Nicholas stared at me, horrified, as if by calling Tatiana an illusion I had committed some awful blasphemy. He needed her to be real, to be his only true friend in the House. It was obvious that he was at least half in love with her. And now I was trying to kill her! His face became stern and his forehead wrinkled in a frown. I could almost imagine his brain churning over this new suggestion from me and frantically seeking grounds to reject it.

The process lasted a long time, with Nicholas staring out into the distance while I waited patiently to field the objections that I knew must come.

Finally, he slowly turned his head towards me, a vague air of triumph on his face.

'You are forgetting two very important things, Marie-Claire,' he said at last. 'The first is that Tatiana was always in colour, real, whereas the illusions were monochrome, based on photographs.

'The second, even more important, is that she was seen by the others and they constantly interrogated me about her, almost obsessively, and searched everywhere for her.'

He paused, pleased with his rebuttal of my theory, and watched me, awaiting my answer.

I suppressed the sigh that I felt rising in me. I didn't like it, but I was about to kill the only person Nicholas could hold on to out of his entire nasty experience at the House.

'All right, Nico, let us deal with your two objections to my theory. If I understood it correctly, your argument is that Tatiana was real because she was different from the other hallucinations – which you are prepared to accept as such – and that she was seen by several people other than yourself. OK?'

He nodded confidently.

'We can deal with your first objection relatively easily. LSD and similar compounds of hallucinogens are known to intensify colours, or rather our perception of them. The reason the other historical persons you saw were monochrome is simply that they were originally "suggested" to your mind by way of old black and white photographs. We have established this, haven't we?'

He nodded again, no doubt wondering where I was going with this.

'Among the few photographs that exist of the adult Tatiana Nicolaevna Romanova is a famous portrait in colour – it was coloured by hand after the original monochrome print was developed. The colours are subdued but produce a subtle, lifelike effect. This is a well-known picture, since it was one of the last to have been taken and shows her as a young adult and looking very beautiful.

'Although all the books had been removed from the library by the time we searched the House, I am convinced that you were shown one containing this very picture. It was put into your subconscious mind in the same way as all the others that we believe were "planted" on you.

'You see, Nicholas, she didn't just appear and disappear like some magic trick; she was *always* with you, and was triggered by your subconscious as a defence whenever times of stress and various drugs disabled your conscious perception.

'You asked her once, how she could so suddenly appear, and do you remember her reply, Nico? She said, "You see me only when you *want* to."'

I paused, wondering whether I had perhaps lost him in the jargon of my profession. Nicholas said nothing, and I could almost hear the cogs whirring in his brain as he struggled to take it all in.

'But, Marie-Claire, your argument is still negated by my second point – she was seen at the séance by six other people, so how could she be only a figment of my imagination?'

I had not forgotten this second argument; indeed, it had initially been very difficult for me to solve.

'But was she, Nicholas? Was she *really* seen or heard by the others?'

Before he could reply, I plunged into the nub of my theory.

'Let's consider this point by point. You say that Anya heard Tatiana's voice in the garden? Well, let me suggest for a moment that Anya heard *your* voice behind the rose arbour, as if talking with someone, yet when she found you, you were alone. She asked who you had been talking to and you described Tatiana, at least the little you knew of her – all facts, incidentally, that could be gleaned from history books. Suppose that Anya reported to Madame Lili that you were not only hallucinating about Tatiana Romanova but were talking to her as well and they decided, there and then, to go along with the illusion, pretending to be concerned and searching the grounds. They generally made a fuss, just to see how far they could go with this new theme.

'Don't forget, Nicholas, you were Dr S.– H.–'s guinea pig. She must have been delighted that one of the hallucinations that she had planted in your mind had seemingly come to life. This was 1968; mind control was in its infancy. Subsequently, every time you encountered Tatiana, and talked to her, they knew – you were certainly under close observation at all times even though it may not have seemed so. My father found wires in your rooms which probably had microphones attached.

'Their deception was brilliantly carried off, with both Anya and Madame Lili appearing very concerned and frantic searches for "Tatiana" taking place.'

I could see that Nicholas was quite shaken by my explanation. I don't think he had ever really seriously considered the possibility that Tatiana was a creation of his subconscious. His face was blank, but I knew his brain was computing my words with an intensity that was making it hurt!

I paused and readied myself for his counter-attack.

Madame Lili must have been pleased with Nicholas as a subject for her experiments because, for all its sophistication, his was an easy mind to read, his thoughts often showing in his facial expressions. His frown relaxed and he looked up at me with the glimmer of a smile. He opened his mouth to speak and I almost said it with him.

'But we all saw her, at the séance!'

I allowed him his moment of triumph and then said, quietly, so as not to seem too pleased with myself, 'You all saw *someone*, Nicholas, I'll grant you that.'

Crestfallen, he asked weakly, 'What do you mean, "someone", Marie-Claire?'

'Let's go over what happened at the séance, step by step, OK?'

He nodded.

'I've read and re-read your account of that event, Nicholas. The chair beside you was empty when the séance began but someone slipped into it in the dark; someone who wore no gloves when she held your hand; someone who smelled strongly of Jasmin de Corse; and, therefore, someone you eventually identified as Tatiana. You got one quick glimpse of her when the light went on for a second and, though her face was averted, you saw her auburn hair from behind; then, in the darkness that followed, she disappeared, to Serge's cry of "Your Highness!"'

'All those factors combined to suggest to you that your partner in the dark was Tatiana. Correct?'

He looked at me but did not answer, just nodded again.

'Now, think back, Nico. Who was missing from that séance?'

He made no answer.

'Natalie, of course!' I triumphed. 'Natalie left the room before the séance on the pretext that the Grand Duchess needed her. I believe that she then changed her dress, took off her gloves, put on an auburn wig and the telltale Jasmin de Corse perfume worn by "Tatiana" and with the complicity of Serge crept back into the room under cover of darkness and sat in the seat next to you. When the light flashed on momentarily she, Natalie, was already on her feet and moving away, her back to you; Serge shouts out "Your Highness" just so there would be no mistake and, again under cover of darkness, he lets her out of the door before dazzling everyone with the electric lights, allowing Natalie to make her exit through the rest of the House.'

Exhausted, I glanced at Nico. He was looking at me, but his eyes were not focused and his face had gone slack as he struggled to take it all in.

He stood up and walked a few paces towards the lake before turning back to me. He still didn't speak, and I wondered how long it would take him to get to the final objection. It didn't take long.

'And later that night, Marie-Claire, who was in my bed?'

But I had sown the seeds of doubt and it sounded in his voice; this was a question more than an objection.

'That, I cannot say, Nico. Remember, you drank a lot of vodka and you describe your sleep as "troubled". Maybe you *dreamt* that you made love to Tatiana, or maybe Natalie continued her deception. I really cannot say. But it does not change my theory. I am certain that you were deceived at the séance and that the subsequent alarm shown by the guests was an example of accomplished acting – with the exception of Serge's "Your Highness", which in my opinion was a bit over the top.'

Nicholas returned to the bench and sat beside me in complete silence, a result I welcomed because it meant that he could find no serious objections to my explanation.

The silence lasted a long time. A cool breeze sprung up and rippled the darkening water of the lake and still Nicholas did not speak. He was touching the hair at the back of his head – a gesture I knew well; it was his habit when concentrating hard on a problem.

From time to time, he looked up and out across the park, seeing nothing, sometimes frowning and sometimes showing his confusion by gently shaking his head. The breeze felt stronger and began to rustle the leaves of the plane trees nearby.

At last Nicholas stood up. 'Shall we go back? I need a drink.'

I went with him, back to the church square, but gently declined the offer of an apéritif, sensing that he really wanted to be alone but was too polite to say so. I had just killed Tatiana and he needed time to get used to that. He kissed me on both cheeks and, as we parted, managed a wan smile, trying to disguise the hurt he must be feeling.

The few minutes it took me to walk home were racked with self-doubt. Had I done the right thing? I really believed that solving this last piece of the puzzle would bring some sort of peace to Nicholas's troubled soul. But it still felt as though I had kicked the crutch out from under a sick and vulnerable man! I had condemned my patient (and my friend) to nights of struggle with his already fragile and perturbed mind, trying to come to terms with the fact that his only friend and saviour at the House was really just another deception, practised on him not by those people who had nothing but contempt for his feelings, but by himself.

Sometimes, the cure can be worse than the disease.

I wrote, in retirement, the epilogue for this English edition of the book, hoping that I had helped Nicholas to live to the full again and to get on with his life without looking back over his shoulder.

But I was wrong.

The week before I submitted this revised edition of our story, Nicholas called me and asked to meet for lunch. Agreeing, I asked him what he was so excited about.

'I've seen her, Marie-Claire!'

I hesitated, not knowing what I should say.

'Who?' I managed, lamely.

'Tatiana, of course!'

We met, and immediately I knew that something was seriously wrong. In spite of Nicholas's odd summons, I still thought it might be some sort of a joke on his part, but in the few weeks since I had last seen him Nicholas had lost weight; his suit hung on him loosely and his shirt had not been pressed. His cheeks were drawn, and his eyes were ringed with black and shone with a light only seen in the seriously demented. Even before I could sit down, he was talking rapidly.

'I've seen her, Marie-Claire, I've seen Tatiana!' he kept repeating.

'Nico, tell me, slowly, all about it.'

'She came to me a few nights ago. At first, I thought it was a dream but it really was Tatiana. She was just as I remembered her. She stayed with me all night. We talked and talked. Now she comes to me often and shares my bed. It's so wonderful. I'm not lonely any more. She said she'd always be with me if I want her and she's promised she'll never leave me again.'

I looked at my friend, not knowing what to say to him. My worst fears were realised and it was as if we were back to square one. At last I found my voice.

'Nicholas, calm yourself. You know that can't be true.'

I spoke as softly as I could but the other diners were staring at us, alarmed by Nicholas's outburst.

'Look, Nico, you remember that I told you that LSD can stay in your system for years, maybe forever, and then suddenly start up again? That's what's happening to you now. You've had a bad trip caused by residual hallucinogens…'

But he was already shaking his head. 'No. No, it's not that; drugs had nothing to do with it. It's the SPACES; the spaces where people get caught up and can never leave. Tatiana explained it all to me but I missed it the first time – didn't grasp it, with all that other stuff going on at the House. That's what frightened Madame Lili, you see; it was something she couldn't control…didn't understand.'

'Spaces?' I repeated mechanically.

'Exactly. Look, Marie-Claire, I'll explain. You see, it's all to do with conceptuality. There is truth and there are lies. There is fact and there is fiction. There is life and there is death. And then there are the spaces in between!'

He looked at me, smiling, pleased with himself that he had resolved all his problems, and eagerly awaiting my reassurance that he was right.

My heart sank. I looked past him out of the window where Parisians were walking by, blissfully unaware of the fear that gripped my heart.

My blood ran cold but he needed an answer. I heard myself saying, 'Of course, Nico. You must introduce her to me.'

'Naturally,' he replied, with a weird sort of smile, reaching out and taking my hand. 'Come home with me; she's waiting there.'

*'The boundaries that divide Life from Death are, at best, shadowy and vague. Who shall say where one ends and other begins?'*

EDGAR ALLEN POE

# Dedication

*'For the most wild yet most homely narrative which I am about to pen, I neither expect nor solicit belief. Mad indeed would I be to expect it, in a case where my very senses reject their own evidence. Yet, mad am I not — and very surely do I not dream. But tomorrow I die, and today I would unburden my soul.'*

EDGAR ALLAN POE

There may still be people alive who were complicit in this macabre tale. If that is so, then it is just possible that, after all these years, they may feel some regret at the hurt they inflicted, though I certainly will not expect any letters of apology and heartfelt sorrow. Such people have no conscience.

Rather, this story is dedicated to the memory of Tatiana Nicolaevna Romanova, brutally murdered before her twentieth birthday.

Her mysterious presence throughout this sad tale has been explained by those who sought to help me (and, indeed, did so) as a figment of my fevered imagination — a by-product of chemically induced hallucinations. If that is so, as well it may be, it has been a very long and convincing 'trip', for she is with me still and I feel her presence beside me now as I write these last few lines. Perhaps now we shall both find peace.

VAN REENAN
September 2017

Tatiana Nicolaevna Romanova

# Acknowledgements

With heartfelt gratitude to the late Dr Marie-Claire Gröller and her father, who saved my sanity and probably my life.

Many thanks to Clare Christian, Anna Burtt, Heather Boisseau and Linda McQueen for believing in me and making this book possible.

To Sue Jeffery, who struggled so valiantly with my scrawl to type the manuscript.

To Patrick Knowles for his beautiful cover design.

To Sara Findlay, Paul Phelps, Vickie Butcher-Phelps, Sarah Weeks-Jones and 'Lady' Polly Aldous for their support and encouragement, without which I would never have completed this book.

And to my daughter Claire and son Michael, for loving such a weird father.

# About the Author

Collin Van Reenan was born in England but has spent considerable time in Western Europe, particularly France. Educated both in Paris and in London, he has had an eclectic selection of jobs and has worked, *inter alia*, as a labourer, driver, teacher, tour guide, immigration officer and police officer (the Met). Bilingual in French and English, he also speaks some Dutch and Arabic and worked until recently as an official police and court interpreter at Bow Street and the Old Bailey, until increasing deafness and a disliking of political correctness prompted him to retire. In 2012, he inherited his family's French title and is the 5th Count Van Reenan, the earlier counts having left France in 1870 after local accusations of vampirism (!).

Currently sharing his time between a small apartment in Paris and his home in Essex, he pursues his interest in the occult and paranormal.

Please email countcollin@gmail.com should you have any information regarding the story or any of the characters discussed in this book.

Join the conversation on Facebook at @thespacesinbetweenbook